I0670447

PIECES OF THE GAME

PIECES OF THE GAME

LEE GIFFORD

CUTTING EDGE

Copyright © 1960 by Lee Gifford

The characters and events portrayed in this book are fictitious. Any similarity to real persons, living or dead, is coincidental and not intended by the author.

No part of this book may be reproduced, or stored in a retrieval system, or transmitted in any form or by any means, electronic, mechanical, photocopying, recording, or otherwise, without express written permission of the publisher.

ISBN-13: 978-1-952138-22-5

Published by
Cutting Edge Publishing
PO Box 8212
Calabasas, CA 91372
www.cuttingedgebooks.com

CHAPTER ONE

It was cold in Wharton's office. Just a few degrees colder than the old man himself. Above the air-conditioning unit that purred like a lazy cat on the window sill, I could see the heat waves rising from the black asphalt roofs across Market Street.

He let me stand. I surveyed the acreage of his kidney-shaped desk while he pretended to ignore me by rattling a few papers, jabbing at them with a fountain pen that rasped harshly. Like Wharton, it was cheap.

There was a ring of frizzled gray hair around the pinched pinkness of his nearly bald head. It looked like a target. A pinched voice squeezed out from the other side of the target. It, too, had a gray ring around it.

"Ready to go, Sheridan?"

"Yeah," I answered. "American-Orient. Four o'clock this afternoon."

"When do you arrive in Manila?" He was busy reading the fine print in a contract, his rimless glasses flashing in grim pursuit of uncrossed "t's" and undotted "i's".

"Friday noon. I'll send you a cable when I arrive at the hotel."

He gave me a quick glance, his mouth pursed up like an old marble bag, and grunted with enthusiasm at my thoughtfulness.

"Did you get your expense money from the cashier?"

"Yeah. I drew a thousand. If I need more you can send it to the Casa Grande Hotel."

He never heard my last sentence. At "a thousand" he had gone into his shock routine, his eyelids fluttering wildly, one trembling, blue-veined hand clutching at his shirt pocket.

"Jim! A thousand! You're not supposed to *buy* any pearls—just make arrangements, set up a pipeline, get the feel of things." His words spilled out, panic-ridden. "Watch your expenses carefully. With a little caution I'm sure you'll be able to turn some of it back in."

"Look," I said, "you know how I feel about this trip; I've had my share of the Philippines—right up to my pearly white teeth. Now I'd like to forget about it. As far as I'm concerned it's over and done with."

I could feel my voice rising as I gripped the front edge of his desk and leaned toward the cold face staring at me. Knowing it was hopeless even as I asked, I tried anyway, reducing the volume with a great effort.

"Why don't you send Bob Cook? He likes to travel—and his expense accounts are only pale imitations of mine."

Wharton blinked slowly, then sighed like a punctured tire. "Because you can speak Spanish like a native..." his voice was monotonous, flat, with the dullness of having gone over the same ground several times, "...because I received specific instructions from the home office to send you on this errand, because I am only general manager in charge of the San Francisco office and you are only an assistant manager. Am I beginning to make myself clear?"

"Yeah," I muttered, yanking a chair up to the desk, uninvited, "like crystals and bells. Now, let's go over my instructions just one last time. I'd hate to arrive in Manila and then forget my lines in this clock-and-dagger melodrama. I'd lose my big chance at an Oscar."

Wharton was not amused. He wouldn't know an Oscar if you pounded him across his skinny slats with one—which, come to think of it, wasn't a bad idea.

Bob Cook spotted me as I left Wharton's office twenty minutes later. He held up two fingers questioningly, then stabbed them at the coffee and doughnuts that had just been brought in by the vendor service. I nodded and entered my office.

In a couple of minutes Bob bounced in and, with practiced routine, pulled out the slide under the top of my desk and set down the cardboard tray. I looked at the fluid in the coffee cup skeptically. It was algae green.

"My God! What is it?"

His puffy fat face swelled with a grin. He loved the identification bit we went through each morning.

"The milk of human kindness—as dispensed by the Great Western Importing Company."

"Socrates never had it so good," I muttered, picking up the paper cup and toasting him with it. "Here's to the youth of Athens—and the babes of Manila."

His eyes expanded and garbled words climbed over the doughnut in his mouth. "No kidding?"

I nodded and peered closely into the coffee. At least nothing was moving in it.

"Didja tell him I'd just as soon go in your place?"

Again I nodded. Then shook my head. "No go."

"Balls!" he said poetically. "Sure as hell woulda been nice to get away from home for a little while. Recharge the batteries—if you know what I mean."

"I know what you mean."

Hopelessly he gave a deep sigh. It was like watching a blimp that had just been shot full of holes.

"Some guys have all the luck. I been here ten years; I'm an account manager. You been here three years; you're next in line for Wharton's job. I had to beg for a job at coolie wages. You they chase to hell-and-gone offering the world on a string. Why? Will you please tell me why?"

I shrugged, feeling sorry for him. I didn't know why. He knew ten times as much about the importing business as I did. Maybe he tried too hard. Maybe he breathed wrong.

He spoke again, tonelessly. "What are you supposed to do in Manila, work on that mahogany contract?"

"Nope. Arrange to put us in the pearl-importing business."

"Hah, hah. Big joke. And you're going to dive for them." He looked up as he swigged another dose of coffee, then slowly put his cup down. "My God, you're serious!"

I didn't answer. The coffee was removing the lining from my throat.

"Pearls!" He was stunned. "But why? We've spent ten years building up a successful business in industrial products—jute, lacquer, lumber. What the devil do we know about marketing pearls?"

"Nothing. But I guess we're about to learn."

His mouth still hung open with shock. Slowly he hinged it together. "It's crazy. Where did he ever get a hare-brained idea like this?"

"Says it came from the home office."

"Hah! He blames the home office for all his trial balloons. If they pan out all right he takes the credit."

"That's why he's a general manager." I broke off a piece of doughnut that was sturdy enough to be used in a hockey game. "If you think the basic idea is screwy, you should hear the trimmings." For his benefit I told him part of the instructions that Wharton had given me. He didn't believe a word of it.

"So help me," I concluded, raising my right hand.

He reached out and helped himself to the other half of my doughnut. "And you don't even know the name of this character you're supposed to meet?"

"Nope. He's to contact me at the Casa Grande Hotel in Manila."

He settled his bulk back into the chair, wiping the crumbs off his face with the back of his hand. Then he chuckled. "It's fantastic! I think you're pulling my leg."

Without answering, I pulled the small pearl from my pocket and dropped it into the ashtray on my desk. It was white, lustrous, about the size of a pea. He stared at it, hypnotized.

I stared at it, too, wondering by what route it had finally ended up here in my possession. There was something phony about the whole business. And I think Wharton knew it. He tried not to show it, but his tidy little mind was as confused as a comptometer that kept coming up with the wrong total.

"Bob," I asked, "are you sure you can't make any wild guess as to who owns this company? Do you have any clue, whatsoever?"

He shook his head. We'd been over this before. "Unh uh. All home-office correspondence, little as it is, goes directly to Wharton. All I know is, I get my check every month, rain or shine." He pushed himself up out of the chair. "Well, back to the oars—unless you've got more?" His tone was hopeful.

I picked up the ashtray, tilting it so the pearl raced about the outer rim. "No. That's it—lock, stock and pearl."

CHAPTER TWO

The engines droned monotonously, and the propellers cut shimmering discs of nothingness out of the thin air. Far below, the blue Pacific was dead calm, providing a mirror for the blinding, raw sun. The empty sea unrolled toward me under the burnished wings of the DC-6 like a blank scroll, and I sat there reading it like an idiot. None of the islands was visible yet and I knew it would be several hours before we started to let down over Luzon. Completely bored, I shoved up from my seat and went down the long aisle to the cocktail lounge.

It was only partially filled and about as full of life as a vacuum chamber. An elderly gent with his wife, both stout, gray and dignified, were sipping at tall glasses filled with Tom Collins. The bracelets clinked on her arm and the ice clinked in her glass each time she bent an elbow.

Across from them an enormously fat individual, wearing tropical whites right down to his suede shoes, was sprawled out in his chair, half-asleep. Which half, I couldn't tell. Without opening his eyes, his hand occasionally groped toward a bottle of beer on the small table beside him and, with the patience of a St. Bernard, labored up and over the mountain of his belly and up-ended a quarter of the bottle into his cavernous throat.

Two Filipino businessmen furnished the only animation as they sat sideways in their seats and chattered softly and volubly. They wore cotton shirts emblazoned with colorful Hawaiian scenes which, judging by the creases, had just been purchased in Honolulu. Frequently their eyes swiveled to enjoy the scenery—which was seated at a corner table at the rear of the lounge.

She seemed totally unconcerned over the expanse of nylon stocking that showed above her knees as she sat, completely engrossed in the book that rested in her lap. Pretty, girl-next-door pretty, she had wide-set brown eyes and honey-colored hair worn long in defiance of the current Italian vogue. A small golden arrow clasped it together in back.

As I dropped into the chair on the opposite side of the corner table, I noted the title of the book: *The Philippines—Land and People*. Well, well. A schoolteacher. Abroad in the wide world during summer vacation. She looked about old enough to be telling fourth graders all about curious Spanish customs.

A small Filipino waiter with glossy, black hair and an immaculately white jacket promptly hove within range.

"May I help you, sir?" His voice was distantly polite, softly modulated.

It seemed like a good time to start polishing up on my Spanish. "*Sí, por favor. Un Barrateaga Cooler.*"

The smile broadened. "*Ah, señor. Perdone usted.* I assumed you were an American."

"You assumed correctly," I answered, still in Spanish. "I thought it wise to practice my Spanish before we land in Manila."

He raised his brows in surprise. "But, *señor*. You could give me lessons. You speak our language superbly."

"That'll get you a nice tip," I grinned. "*Como se llama usted?*"

"Arturo, *señor. Servidora de usted.*"

As Arturo left I fished out a cigarette from my shirt pocket, feeling the girl's eyes lift for an instant to regard me speculatively. I met her glance as I probed about for an ashtray, the black cadaver of a dead match between my fingers. She smiled briefly and slid the ashtray across to a more convenient position. I nodded my thanks and, excavating the entire package of cigarettes, held it out to her questioningly. For an instant she hesitated, then took one with a frowning effort to thank me in Spanish.

"Muchas gracias, señor."

Her accent was terrible. I grinned as I realized she was unaware I could speak English.

"De nada," I answered gravely.

She glanced back at the volume that had fallen shut in her lap. Taking it for a well-bred gesture of dismissal, I leaned my head against the back of my chair and closed my eyes with a relaxed sigh.

Wharton's dry voice came back to me reading that ridiculous letter of instruction. It sounded like something right out of a spy thriller. "I am the buyer, not the seller." And the response: "I have the black, not the white." And that bit about the Casa Grande. It stretched coincidence far beyond any limit of elasticity. Who would want to lure me, by such quaintly devious means, back to a piece of my past? And why? It had been thirteen years ago. Most of them were dead—I had seen them die. Or they were scattered to the four winds, across the seven seas. Nick Borrelli—drowned. Joe Price—shot. Guido and Esteban—executed. The parade of ghostly figures continued.

There couldn't be any connection. It defied logic, perverted sanity. I had built a monument out of two pounds of bricks—without mortar.

But I couldn't stamp out the whirling kaleidoscope of memories; the green hell of Bataan's jungles, the numbing shock of defeat on the white rock of Corregidor, the roaring engine of a PT boat that exploded in death and fire.

And Tulana. Quiet, shy, beautiful Tulana. After the war, I had spent futile, fruitless months searching for her, turning Manila upside down by its filthy, teeming roots. But no one knew—or would say. No one in the mountain village where she was born, no one in the waterfront dives, no one in the swanky night spots where she could have been singing under a different name. I finally admitted defeat. Either she was no longer alive or, for some reason of her own, she did not wish to be found by an exhausted, war-weary ex-lieutenant by the name of Jim Sheridan.

Back to UCLA. Finish my courses in Oriental cultures and archaeology. A job in San Francisco as assistant professor, teaching in the daytime, trying to forget in the darkness of the night. Then a phone call from Wharton and a sudden, desperate plunge into a new life that had helped wash away the past.

So, here I am on my reluctant way back to Manila. To the Casa Grande. Like they say—it's a diminutive sphere.

I was jarred from my reverie by the sound of a clinking glass at my elbow. Arturo had delivered my drink. As I pulled myself up and reached for it thirstily, I saw the girl's innocent brown eyes fixed on me anxiously. Apparently she was waiting for an answer.

"Perdons usted, ah, señorita," I apologized, quickly checking for signs of wedding rings.

She gave the book in her lap a hopeless wave of her hand, indicating there was something she didn't understand and wanted to ask me about.

"Habla...usted...ingles?" she asked ponderously.

I blinked. What made her think I didn't? Then I recalled my conversation with Arturo and the fact that it was all in Spanish.

"Yes," I began. "May I..."

"Darn it all," she interrupted, "I *knew* I should have studied Spanish before I set out on this safari!"

I tried again, "But I do speak..."

"You'll have to be patient with me, that's all," she continued. "If you enunciate clearly I can keep up with you."

"But..."

"Now," she folded her hands on top of her book and, furrowing the lovely smoothness of her brow, plunged gamely into a labored imitation of the foreign language. "Now—about Manila," she said brightly. "You have been there, yes?"

"But, *sí*," I sighed hopelessly. "Eeet ees mucho city, yes?"

She blinked but didn't comment on my compromise between the two languages. "I've never been there. But I've read so much about the tropics. It must be wonderful to live where the trade winds blow and the flowers bloom all year 'round. Manila never has snow, does it?"

"Oh, but no, *señorita*," I answered enthusiastically. "Six months of dust. Six months of mud."

Her brown eyes grew impossibly round as she stared at me, absorbing this distressing bit of information. Then suddenly, deep dimples appeared in her cheeks and her soft, full lips quirked in a brilliant smile.

"You're teasing me," she stated matter-of-factly. "What is your name? *Como se llamo ...*"

I interrupted, lifting my hand to spare her the effort of translation.

"Diego," I answered, giving her the Spanish equivalent of Jim. "And yours?"

"Ellen. Ellen Roberts."

"Ah. Elena." With serious formality I gave her a courtly bow. I must have overdone it. A quick flash of suspicion scampered across her smooth features, like a small, lost rain cloud. It swiftly disappeared in the sunny brightness of her disposition. The more we talked, the more I became aware that this was quite a girl—as intelligent as she was attractive. It seemed a shame that she, like youth, also had to be wasted on children. She asked dozens of penetrating questions about the Philippines—all about the habits and habitats of the Igorots, for instance. It fortified my deduction that she was a schoolteacher and I decided to impress her with my cleverness.

"You go back to the school after the summer is over, yes?"

Again those long lashes swept down in a startled blink.

"You are the schoolteacher. You teach the children, yes?"

Suddenly the dimples reappeared. A wondrous transformation as she smiled with a smile as warm as an electric blanket.

"Oh. Whatever made you guess that?" Abruptly, she turned her head to peer out the window as something caught her eye. "Look! We're over land. It must be Luzon."

I sat back, smiling to myself in smug satisfaction as I wondered why schoolteachers never wanted to admit their occupation when on vacation trips. Well, if she wasn't impressed by my clairvoyance I certainly was.

The customs routine was the same, endless exasperation designed by pompous bureaucrats that infested every port of entry in the world. But the Filipinos had added nothing to it that couldn't be cut short by the length of a five-dollar bill. In fifteen minutes I was out on the street in front of the customs building and, for the first time, it really sunk in that I was back in Manila. It washed over me in a hot, humid wave. The heavy breath of the tropics—scented with fish, moldy wooden buildings, a million people who seldom bathed unless they happened to fall into the Pasig River. It had been a long time.

I turned to the boy who was hustling my bags and told him to cut a taxicab out of the honking herd that milled in front of us like a steel stampede. As I watched him go into action, a familiar voice spoke at my elbow. It was Ellen. I looked at her in surprise.

"How did you get through customs so fast?" It was impossible that she could have been such a sophisticated traveler.

She was breathless, her face pink with exertion. But she managed a mildly acid retort.

"They didn't ask me to declare my fake Spanish accent," she said with a mock glare. She tried for a moment to hold back, but then exploded in a sudden, merry laugh. Those dimples were wonderful. "But it's all right, Diego. I forgive you."

She promptly dismissed the matter and stared, wide-eyed, toward the raucous, seething millrace of automobiles.

"How do you trap one of those things?" she asked forlornly.

"I've got a beater out there now," I said, pointing to my porter. "When he gets one close enough, we give it a flanking attack. But you've got to be quick—they're anti-pedestrian."

She looked up at me gratefully. "Oh, would you? My Spanish is so rotten…"

For some reason I decided against telling her they spoke better English than most Americans.

"Why certainly," I assured her. "I'm going across town, anyway. I'll drop you off wherever you like. Where are you staying?"

"At the Casa Grande."

I stared at her in astonishment. It wasn't a place where schoolteachers stayed.

"Good Lord!" I muttered.

"What?" She tilted her head toward me politely.

"Nothing. Just assumed you'd be staying at the Manila Hotel."

The cab driver also thought she should go to the Manila Hotel. He said so, loudly and at great length. After I reassured him in his conclusion that all Americans are not sane—in fact, some not even wealthy—he threw his arms in the air with exasperation. With a metallic shout of protest, the cab clanked into gear and pitched us against our seats as it roared out into the traffic with suicidal indifference to right-of-way.

Ellen, sitting forward and pulling her skirt back down over her knees, turned to me with a smile. "What was *that* all about? I thought you two would end up in a duel."

I shrugged. "We were agreeing with each other that you should stay at the Manila Hotel. I'm at the Casa myself."

"Well, if that's agreement I'd sure hate to hear an argument!"

"It got a little involved. I took your side."

"My hero!" She sighed happily as she gave me a big, brown-eyed, melting look. "I think it's just wonderful, though—both of us at the same hotel. At least I'll know somebody."

I sighed to myself. Everybody seemed to learn the facts of life except the teachers. Feeling a bit gauche, I started to warn her about life in a strange town, but she interrupted by putting a restraining hand on my arm and delicately sniffing the air. I grinned, waiting for her reaction. I should have expected that it wouldn't be what I expected.

She exhaled with a deep sigh of appreciation. "Isn't it wonderful? Just like perfume. Hibiscus, oleanders, freshly cut grass..."

Startled, I gingerly gave the air another try. By golly, she was right!

"What is the Casa Grande like? Is it nice?" There was a faint trace of worry beneath her light manner.

Casually I pulled out a cigarette, lit it, and let it hang from the corner of my mouth. I talked from the other corner.

"The Far East is full of joints like the Casa Grande. It's international, cosmopolitan. You want a few ounces of heroin, you can find an Egyptian smuggler. You need a few guns for a revolution, you can find an American renegade. You want a nice young Chinee girl, you can find a white-slaver."

She looked at me for a moment, then slumped her shoulders in resignation and gave me a disgusted voice.

"Now you cut that out!" she said grimly. "You've taken me for one ride already. That's your quota for the day."

"I feel rejected," I muttered meekly.

The Casa Grande was a rococo monstrosity of uncertain age. Unknown builders. Indefinite pedigree. It was located on the edge of "old town" where decaying respectability meets the respectably decadent. Pink stucco towers, undernourished minarets, and wrought-iron balconies effectively disguised the original architect's intent with awesome thoroughness.

Ellen gasped as our cab clawed to a halt before the ornate doorway. "Good heavens! Is this it?" She looked at me with skepticism, suspecting trickery.

I nodded as a bearded Sikh sauntered out through the doorway and stood in the shade of the awning. She stared at his turban as if expecting a cobra to crawl out of it.

"This is it." I relented at the sight of her worried look. "It may look like the hatching ground of gargoyles, but actually it's very clean. Well run, by local standards. And don't let the exotic appearance of its clientele scare you. That fellow is probably a traveling salesman for a burlap-bag company."

She took in a deep breath, still regarding him dubiously. "If this place is full of traveling salesmen, I think I prefer your earlier description."

The alarm in her face quickly gave way to a muffled squeal of pleased surprise when we entered the spacious lobby. It was cool and relaxing. Soft light filtered through the skylights high overhead. With potted plants everywhere, it was like walking into a botanical exhibit—glossy, dark green rubber trees, willowy palms arching gracefully toward the ceiling, pale green hydrangea bushes with pale pink blossoms.

Across the glistening mosaic of the tile floor moved a desultory scattering of small, dusky-skinned Filipinos, Chinese with darting black eyes, slow-gaited Near Easterners in long, flowing white robes. Above them, suspended from the ceiling, large four-bladed fans stirred the faintly scented air with a lethargic hum.

As we approached the desk, from which a fat Chinese clerk watched us with all the excitement of a bronze Buddha, I suddenly felt Ellen's fingernails dig into my upper arm. Yipping as I unbent her frightened clutch, I looked around to see what had caused her alarm. I didn't blame her.

Roaring toward us, like a pirate boarding a ship, was a giant of a man. With his lips pulled back in a grimace, his swarthy face made his teeth stand out like piano keys. Bushy, black hair flowed in all directions. Twin mustachios drooped three inches under either side of his huge nose. Ellen barely avoided his muscular arms as he grabbed me in a rib-cracking embrace.

"*Sacré! Sacré!* Eet's *mon ami.* Monsieur Sheridan!" He bussed me on the cheeks and held me out like a rag doll for inspection.

I fought my way back to the floor with a grin and rubbed my arms. "It's what is left of him. How are you, Jacques? It has been a long time, *n'est-ce pas?*"

It had been a dozen years since I had last seen Jacques Costeau, and for the next five minutes he tried to bridge the gap of time by a steady barrage of questions in French. Not too fluent in the language, I did my best to keep up with him. After the initial explosion settled down, I turned to Ellen who had taken a protected position behind my shoulder. She smiled uncertainly as I introduced them.

"Ellen," I said, "this is Jacques Costeau, owner of Casa Grande, and the biggest-hearted rogue in the Orient."

As she took a tentative step forward, I turned to the huge Frenchman. "And this is Ellen Roberts. We came over on the same plane..." I got no further.

Jacques, who was put together with a series of short fuses, exploded again. This time it was like a string of firecrackers. More than slightly mystified at his delighted acceptance of this complete stranger, I waited for his powder to give out.

"But Jim, this is *merveilleux!*" He rose from his elegant bow, his mustachios swinging silkily. "Truly, this is my day of good fortune, eh?"

Ellen gave me a slightly pink look. She wasn't accustomed to being kissed on the hand. At least that's how I interpreted it.

"I am so pleased. The Casa Grande has nevair been honored by so lovely a creature." With a delighted bellow, he crushed my shoulder good-naturedly. "Ah, but you two must have had much to talk about on your trip to Manila, is it not true?"

I shoved my shoulder back into place. "Would you mind telling me what this is all about?" I felt a bit peevish.

But he turned back to Ellen. "*Mais, mademoiselle,*" he apologized, "I am so rude. You must be fatigued from your long journey. And Monsieur Sheridan and I have so many years to account for that I restrain myself with difficulty."

Ellen gave me a suspiciously sweet smile as Costeau whirled lightly as a ballet dancer, clapping his hands imperiously.

"*Attention*, Pablo!"

From the mezzanine a small Filipino boy with dancing black eyes scrambled down the staircase and seized Ellen's luggage. Costeau regarded him fondly.

"A good lad," he informed us. "And very smart. I am teaching heem the English."

I was still looking at Ellen. "Well, please teach me something. How come you know Miss Roberts? She has never been in Manila before."

Costeau looked from one of us to the other, settling on me with a puzzled expression. "But you do not know? She is to work for me. She has consented to be our new singer in the Casa Grande Casino!"

My mouth opened. Finally I made it. "Singer!"

Ellen had started to follow Pablo toward the stairs. Still only a few feet away, she tossed me a smug look.

"See you later—Diego!"

Very confused, Jacques mirrored my blank face. "Diego?"

"Those lousy dimples," I muttered.

We talked a little longer. About people we once knew. About the rebuilding of the city. About old times. I wanted to ask him one question very badly—and he knew it. But every time I led up to it he slid off on another tangent with skillful adroitness. Finally, realizing I was tired, he went off to find Pablo to take' care of my bags. I registered at the desk and remembered to wire Wharton. At the foot of the broad marble staircase I met Jacques coming down, and I couldn't put it off any longer.

"Jacques, tell me—have you ever heard what became of Tulana?"

The lines in his seamed face deepened. His glance slid quickly over my face and he stared at a point somewhere behind me. Slowly he shook his head.

"I am sorry, *mon ami*. But sometimes it is best ..." He stopped, then shook his head with curt finality. "No. I do not know where she can be found."

I tried to read his opaque eyes but he turned away from me and went on down the stairs. I followed his shambling gait with bewilderment. He was lying. I knew he was lying.

CHAPTER THREE

I t was the same old room I had occupied so many years ago. And the same air I had once breathed was still in it. I pulled the string to the overhead fan. The gears meshed with a groan of protest and the wooden blades wobbled uncertainly, as if not knowing what was expected of them. Pablo dumped my bags on the floor unceremoniously and opened the louvered doors that led onto the balcony.

Deftly catching the coin I flipped to him, he gave me an ear-to-ear grin and aimed his finger across the patio to the room on the opposite side.

"Her room, *señor*—it is over there."

I missed the boat. "Whose?"

"The beautiful singer. Miss Roberts." He sighed at my lack of enterprise. "I thought you'd like to know, *señor*."

My playful swing at his behind missed by a foot. "Get the hell out of here, you little Peeping Pablo. Go find me some ice water."

I waited until he had closed the door behind him, then ambled out onto the balcony. The shades on the opposite side were drawn.

The garden in the patio below me had grown with tropical lushness over the years. To my left, against the high stuccoed wall that stretched between the two wings of the hotel, the little banyan tree I remembered now reached up to the tilted roofs. Flowering vines crawled up the Moorish columns of the veranda and clung to the second-floor railing with tenacious grip. The heady scent of oleander, hibiscus, orchids mingled with the cooling spray that shot skyward from the central pool to form a perfumed, iridescent rainbow. A couple of parakeets eyed me beadily from the stone seat that encircled the pool. Standing my ground staunchly, I eyed them back.

It was impossible to avoid thinking of Tulana as I took in each familiar detail. It had been our favorite rendezvous. Every night, after she had finished with her singing in the casino, she would come out into the patio. And I would be waiting. Right there where those two impertinent parakeets were sitting. And I would have two tall drinks waiting. Her eyes would still be shining from the excitement of singing, her cheeks warm to the touch. And she would throw her head back, looking up at the stars, and inhale deeply of the sweet, night air. Sometimes the distant strumming of a mandolin would drift out to us from the casino, caressing the melodies of soft Spanish songs. Sometimes she would sing for me in her husky, low voice.

For a moment I succumbed to the poignant memory, felt the surge of tingling excitement stirring within me. It was too real. Then suddenly I felt exhausted. As though I had already lived one life and now was forced to live another. I went back into my room and threw myself down on the bed, ignoring the unpacked suitcases still waiting where Pablo had left them. It was only four blinks to blankness.

I had intended to sleep only until dinner time, but since I'm quite thorough about my sleeping, I wasn't too surprised to awaken and find the golden luminescence of a tropical moon streaming across the floor like an orange carpet. I sat up on the edge of the bed, wondering what had awakened me. Finally I grabbed it from the edge of subconsciousness. It was the door. Someone had rapped softly, then rattled the knob.

"Yeah," I answered through a mighty yawn. "Who is it?"

There was no answer. I yawned again. It could have been ten, twenty minutes ago that my visitor had tried to awaken me. I had no way of knowing. Picking my shirt off the high bedpost, I slung it on, fumbling at the buttons in the semidarkness as I went to the door. Sticking my head out into the hallway, I checked both directions. No one. Clicking the door shut I returned to the bed and sat down to put on my shoes, sticking my feet out into the rectangle of moonlight to tie the laces. The patch of light suddenly disappeared into blackness. Startled, I looked up toward the patio doorway.

Framed in the opening, totally eclipsing the moon, was an immensely fat figure. He swayed slightly in complete silence, like a dirigible at a mooring tower. I could hear his short, labored gasps for air as he looked searchingly into the darkness of my room. Irritation overcoming my momentary fear, I picked up one of my shoes and hefted it in my hand.

"All right," I said sharply. "If you're not Peter Pan you'd better talk fast."

He cast off from his mooring, shoving his fat stomach further into the room on stubby, elephantine legs. As he turned toward me, the moonlight fell on his face exposing small eyes folded deep in puffy rolls of flesh. His head was porcelain smooth. Not even eyebrows separated his forehead from his face.

"You are…Mr. Sheridan?" He spoke between gasps in a shuddering whisper and his eyes continually skittered from me, to the dark shadows of the room, to the patio doorway.

"Yes, damn it. What the hell is this all about?"

"Are you…alone?"

I gritted my teeth while an uncontrollable tremor in the muscle of my arm bounced the shoe against my palm without much help from me. "What the devil is it to you?" I demanded.

I could hear him pumping air into his chest for more conversation. Finally he got up enough pressure.

"I apologize profusely…for the manner of my entrance… but, I assure you…it was necessary. When you did not answer my knock I assumed you were out…so I gained entrance to the balcony through an empty room … and came in to await your arrival."

"Good thinking." I started to put on my other shoe. "You can get the hell out through the door."

He acknowledged my graciousness by suddenly thrusting out a hand. "I am Rudolph Tessa."

I ignored the quivering fingers. Shaking them would have been like trying to land a wet fish.

"Look, Tessa," I snarled with complete exasperation, "I've never heard of you, I don't care who you are, and I can't imagine anything we might have in common to discuss. Now get out of here fast, *muy pronto, rapidamente.*"

For some reason, nothing I said seemed to register.

"I understand you are interested … in buying pearls?"

That one jolted me. Odd as it may sound, I had almost forgotten why I was in Manila. I had taken the whole thing so lightly—actually, so unbelievingly—that I had banished any thought of a genuine, dyed-in-the-wool "contact" for the whole ridiculous project.

"Perhaps," I said slowly. "But this sure as the devil is an odd way to sell them."

He made an awkward, placating gesture. "I assure you, Mr. Sheridan … it is necessary."

As I got up and started for the floor lamp, his voice rose in an alarmed squeal of panic. "Please. Please—no lights, I beg of you."

With a sigh of resignation I went back and sat down on the bed, waving him into a chair. Gratefully he wedged himself into it. A long-handled shoe spoon would have helped.

"All right," I gave in, "what's the pitch?"

He rubbed his hands together nervously. "I believe, Mr. Sheridan, that you have … a white pearl to show me."

I grinned to myself in the darkness. Fairy tales do come true. "I'm the buyer, not the seller," I said.

Sure enough, he completed the litany. "And I have the black, not the white."

Slowly, still not believing, I pulled my wallet from under the pillow, opened the coin compartment, and removed the small, white pearl. Holding it out in the palm of my hand, it beamed like a tiny satellite.

With great ceremony, my corpulent visitor excavated in the depths of his pocket and dredged up a bit of tissue paper. He unwrapped it and dropped into my hand a small black pearl. Except for color they were perfectly matched.

"O.K.," I said. "Now what do we do … mate them?"

With a great huffing and puffing, he peeled the chair off his backside and stood up. "My principal … as you now have reason to believe … is exceedingly circumspect. If you will kindly meet me in two hours at the Lido … a small waterfront bar on the docks … I will take you to him."

I knew the Lido. It was about as popular as bubonic plague, and just as sanitary.

"Look," I said, "I like to play games as well as the next guy—but not when I don't know the rules. Who am I dealing with? Why all the two-bit melodrama?"

He shook his head as his eyes skittered toward the doorway. "I am very sorry, Mr. Sheridan … but I do not make the rules, either. *Adios.*"

For all his bulk he managed to disappear out onto the balcony so fast that I was left flat-footed, as it were, still seated on the edge of the bed. Suddenly feeling unclean, I shucked off my shoes again and went into the bathroom, where I turned on the shower faucet and let the water run as I stripped off my clothes.

The plumbing wasn't up to par, but it worked after a fashion. Although I had turned it on full blast, no water appeared until after the pipes had sucked in a hollow, rasping sigh and shuddered in mortal agony. It finally spewed forth a promising sample, then, working itself up to full pitch, shot out a geyser-like torrent accompanied by a hammering airlock that sounded like a maddened machine gun. Before I got the spray properly adjusted, I was tone deaf. Which was probably a good thing. I'm a shower-singer.

Taking my time, I luxuriated in a thorough soaking and eventually climbed out feeling completely renovated. I dried off, admired my candid brown eyes, combed my hair, worried about the streaks of gray at the temples—and jumped two feet when a heavy fist started pounding on the hall door. I went back into the bedroom and snarled at the door.

"All right. All right. Who is it, and what do you want?"

The answer was curt, authoritative. *"Policia."*

Startled, it took me a moment to find my voice. What the devil could they want with me? "Keep your shirt on a minute," I finally yelled. They didn't. All during the time I selected a suitable wardrobe they continued their infernal pounding. It was interspersed with frequent comments designed to help me expedite matters. I finally got to the door and opened it a few degrees.

In the hall were two gendarmes. Their baggy, khaki uniforms were soaked through at the shoulders with perspiration. Olive-skinned faces were set in grim lines as they glared at me. Behind them I could see heads poked out curiously from all the doors in the hall.

"You will come with us, please," one of them said.

"Why?"

"It is not to our knowledge," said the beefier one.

"Adios, then," I answered, starting to close the door. "When it is to your knowledge, come back and we'll discuss it."

"Mr. Sheridan, it is wise not to resist." He pushed against the door with a meaty paw.

I was getting a bit irritated. And I resisted, bracing the door with my foot. "Look, fellows. Let me get this through your skulls. I don't move until I get a simple, lucid explanation. Who the hell do you think you are, anyway?"

Apparently the corporal was accustomed to pinching pick-pockets and street walkers. My attitude of outraged innocence was something new to him and he reacted obviously out of character. Reducing his leverage on the door, he spoke in more reasonable tones.

"There is a dead man beneath your balcony. Captain Gomez would like to discuss the matter with you."

I gaped at him, letting the door swing wide. "What!" Snappy lines like that are born—not made.

There was a small group clustered about the rumpled heap of clothing on the tiles of the patio. They were all from the Manila Police Department. Some were measuring things with tape rules. Two photographers were snapping flash pictures. A white-haired man in a black suit was writing in a notebook. At his feet was a doctor's bag.

As I was marched up between the two cops, one of the group detached himself and turned toward me. He was nattily dressed in an officer's cap and a pressed uniform. He drilled me with a pair of gray eyes that could split diamonds at fifty paces, and pointed a finger at the formless mound.

"Do you know this man, Mr. Sheridan?"

I did. It was Rudolph Tessa—completely and permanently dead. He looked much smaller. I also knew enough about tropical jails not to risk even a temporary visit. The police had a tendency to forget why they jugged you until their memories were stimulated by green bank engravings—but Captain Gomez looked suspiciously, and unreliably, honest.

I shook my head. "Who is he?"

Uncomfortably, his eyes rested on mine for a long moment, then he dropped his arm with a sigh.

"You arrived in Manila this afternoon?"

"Yes."

"For what reason did you come to Manila?"

"My company sent me to arrange for the importing of pearls."

"And what is the name of your company?"

"The Great Western Importing Company."

"You have been to Manila before?"

"Yes."

"How long ago?"

"1940. And through the war. I was captured on Corregidor."

"Oh."

After that I noticed a slight softening in his manner, but he was still quite businesslike. He looked up toward the balcony.

"Would you point out your room, please."

I pointed. It was about forty feet back along the balcony from the point above Tessa's body.

Captain Gomez nodded, clenching his jaw with tired hopelessness. "The room directly above is empty. I am sorry, but we have to question all the occupants."

"I understand. It's all right."

For a moment he stood, lost in thought. I just stood. Then he spoke again. "His name was Rudolph Tessa. He was knifed in the back and pushed over the balcony." From his pocket he pulled out a small square of tissue paper.

"Would this have any significance to you?"

I shook my head, feeling guilty. "No."

His gimlet eyes bored into mine again. "Mr. Sheridan, have you ever heard of 'The Barracuda'?"

This time I was genuinely surprised. "'The Barracuda'? No. I assume you don't mean a fish?"

"I certainly do not!"

Apparently I was the last witness for they finally drifted away, taking the lifeless hulk with them. The case of Rudolph Tessa had become simply another minus statistic in the Philippine population figures. I was hungry, but I needed a drink far worse.

❧   ❧   ❧

The casino was a thick, blue haze kept in a large, low-ceilinged room just off the lobby. Devoted to the fine arts of dining, drinking, and listening to performers make noises from a tiny, spotlighted ring, it was designed for intimacy in spite of its size. Its many floor levels presented a tricky obstacle course in the murky gloom; its dim chandeliers, suspended from the frescoed ceiling by heavy brass chains, scarcely gave enough light to fix a navigable course. And the steady cacophony of a small orchestra which leaned heavily on kettle drums, pounded with a persistent, almost ominous, undertone.

As always, it was crowded. I elbowed my way past dark-skinned East Indians bandaged in top-heavy turbans, shorter Chinese merchants with glittering rings on their fingers who managed to remain watchfully sober in spite of astonishing alcoholic intake, and, of course, the alert, quick-moving Filipinos who, by contrast, seemed like happy children with their constant barrage of magpie chatter. And all the beautiful women of the Orient—dressed to the hilt in evening gowns, attentive to their escorts while covertly window-shopping on the side. I decided my thirst was a lonesome thirst.

Maneuvering for a space at the bar, I ordered a double shot of bourbon with a stiff slug of water for a chaser. While I waited for my medicine, the orchestra throbbed its way into a medley of rhumbas, the drummer brilliantly carrying the ball as his black face glistened beneath a tall, red fez.

The first drink went down like water.

"Another of the same," I told the bartender, "but this time dilute it with a little ice."

I sipped on the second drink, half-listening to the music as I took stock of my situation. With my contact, Rudolph Tessa, now resting in peace, the devious trail seemed to have come to an abrupt end. Well, tomorrow I would wire San Francisco and ask Wharton for instructions. Maybe he'd like me to go opal hunting in Australia. As I negotiated for a third glass, I saw Jacques

Costeau coming toward me from the far end of the bar. I gave him a grin as he approached, about to offer a drink, but he turned a cool, blank stare in my direction and without pausing continued unhurriedly on his way. I gaped at the back of his tuxedo as he moved through the crowd and out of sight. What the devil was eating him?

I suffered deeply for all of thirty seconds. The orchestra had moved into the slow, throbbing strains of "Begin the Beguine." The trumpets were muted hauntingly. Slowly, the curtain behind them was raised, and before the black velvet backdrop stood an astonishingly beautiful girl, her superb figure outlined in a sheath of white silk. Haughtily erect, she tilted back her golden halo of lustrous hair and began to sing, her rich contralto filling the room with a mesmerizing spell.

I stopped breathing as the seething conversational murmur of the casino faded to a trancelike silence. They must have felt the same cold chills crawling up their spines that I did. This, believe it or not, was the same girl I had nearly ignored on the plane just a few hours earlier.

When the curtain came down, the audience applauded until the chandeliers vibrated. I was too stunned to lift my hands.

I was on my fourth drink—an anemic, single shot—when she suddenly appeared at my side, bringing those lovely dimples with her. She was more softly beautiful, and more fuzzily beautiful, than ever.

"Hi, teacher," I grinned.

"Hi, Diego," she gave me a searching look. "Was it that bad?"

"Was what how bad?" I was a little confused.

She smiled faintly, shaking her head. "I have twenty minutes until my next number..."

Realizing that we were standing somewhat awkwardly at the bar, I apologized and led her to a small table in an alcove. She ordered plain soda. For variety, I ordered bourbon—mixed. As our waiter disappeared she gave me an odd look, her head tilted to one side.

"Mr. Costeau has been telling me a lot about you," she said.

"I'm flattered—but since when have I become the object of conversation?"

"I asked him," she said simply, "when we were having dinner together this evening. We hoped you would join us, but you were still asleep—weren't you?"

I was having difficulty keeping up. "Weren't I what?"

"Asleep."

Maybe it was me. Or the unbearable heat of the casino. But the conversation seemed quite unhinged. Her words came from a great distance.

"Mr. Costeau said you could speak seven languages... that you were looking for someone who once meant a great deal to you... that you had a terrible experience with the Japanese during the war... Mr. Costeau said he doesn't really believe you're here to buy pearls..."

I brought myself back into focus with great difficulty.

Her voice went on. "What do you suppose that note meant that they found on that poor man?"

"Note? What note?"

She gave me an odd look. "You mean you really don't know? It was stuck on that knife." She shuddered. "It said: 'To all who would search the depths of Caballo Bay, this is your treasure.' It was signed 'The Barracuda.'"

"'The Barracuda'?" I frowned, wondering where I had heard that before. Oh, yeah. Captain Gomez. But even more mystifying was the reference to Caballo Bay. I knew what had once been there, but... no... it was impossible after all these years.

Ellen had a very strange expression as she gazed at me. Half admiration, half fear. I didn't deserve either.

"Jim." She hesitated, then plunged ahead. "Jim, *are* you 'The Barracuda'?"

I laughed. I was suffocating. I had to get out into the fresh air. But I laughed, unable to control myself. It was hysterical, hilarious. I was just a poor fish.

Ellen stood up as the orchestra came to life, looking at me worriedly. Like a gentleman fish, I swam upright.

"That's my cue," she said. "See you later?"

"Yeah. See you later." I watched the wondrous swaying of her hips as she walked toward the stage. Then abruptly I headed for the nearest exit.

The small park across the street from the hotel was a haven of quiet darkness. Sounds of the city filtered faintly through the thick branches of the bushes. A miniature jungle of slender palms arched up into the blackness of the soft night. Except for the faint rustlings of tiny animals traveling incognito through the flower beds, there was no life in the park. I didn't add much to the sum total.

My feet scratched faintly in the gravel as I shuffled along the winding paths. Gradually the cooler night air dissolved the misty dizziness that enveloped me. It was like taking a pliofilm bag off my head. I dropped onto a wooden bench, stretched my feet out comfortably, and tried to reassemble the bits of conversation I had had with Ellen. Somehow my end of it lacked brilliancy. But what had she said? Something about Costeau thinking I was a fish buyer, and he wanted to sell me a barracuda. No, that didn't seem quite right...

As I jiggled the fragments around into a different order, I became aware of a rustling of leaves. I was surprised. There was more of a breeze inside King Tut's burial chamber than there was in the park. I turned to investigate—and a large, blunt instrument smashed into my head. It was like a graceful swan dive into an empty swimming pool. I went right through the bottom into cloying blackness...

CHAPTER FOUR

My eyelids were shutters on a summer cottage nailed shut until spring. My mouth was as dry and dusty as an unswept porch, and someone had built a new dormer that bulged out over my left ear. There was also construction work going on inside my head. A thousand tiny men with pickaxes were digging a tunnel that would soon connect my right and left ears.

I groaned and rolled over on my side, feeling beads of sweat roll down my cheeks. They tickled. I opened one shutter experimentally and a shaft of blazing sunlight streaming through an open porthole skewered my brain like shish-kabob. Groaning, I sat up, swinging my legs over the side of the bunk, and held my head in my hands.

Faint sounds drifted between my fingers; the squalling meows of seagulls as they wheeled and dived in the azure sky, the murmuring slurp of water against the hull, the rubbing squeak of rope as it tautened and relaxed with the gentle heel of the ship. Occasionally voices floated by. I couldn't make out the words, or even the sex.

My stockinged feet were planted deep in the nap of a pale beige carpet that stretched from bulkhead to bulkhead. A long, low chest of drawers of burnished mahogany gleamed with a polish that reflected colorful Japanese prints complementing the paneled walls. Directly across from me was a small, wood-slatted door. I struggled up, waded through the carpet, and pushed it open. It was a tiny lavatory, gleaming with black onyx and brilliant brass splendor. Obviously, I was on a mighty fancy scow.

The cold water treatment washed away most of the fog and, except for the feeling that I had been pounded, feet first, through the eye of a needle, I was in remarkably good shape. My jacket, pants and white shirt were neatly hung in the wardrobe, my shoes side by side beneath them. Damned if the shoes weren't polished!

While buttoning my shirt, I went to the porthole and looked out. Five or six miles of sparkling blue water separated me from the skyline of Manila. Off to the left I could just barely catch a glimpse of the green jungles of Bataan. There were no ships within sight.

I finished dressing, then tentatively tried the latch that opened the cabin door. It turned easily and I found myself in a narrow, teak-paneled passageway. At one end, a white steel ladder led upwards. Through the open hatch I could see a gaily striped canvas billowing gently in a soft breeze.

As I moved to the ladder a small Japanese cabin boy, clad in stiffly starched white jacket and trousers, descended in swift silence. His eyes showed no surprise as he hugged the bulkhead to let me by. I stopped directly in front of him and pinned him to the wall by placing an arm on either side of his shoulders.

"Whose ship is this?" I demanded brusquely.

"I am sorry," he answered in Japanese. "I do not understand."

Before I had a chance to rephrase my question in Japanese, he slipped under my arm and ran down the passageway. Exasperated, I watched him disappear, then turned and mounted the ladder.

It was pleasantly cool topside. A large fiber mat covered most of the aft portion of the deck under the shade of the fluttering stripes of the awning. Several bamboo chairs were scattered about at strategic intervals. Only one of the chairs was occupied.

He had the same cool hauteur in his obsidian eyes. The same thin-lipped quirk of distant amusement. His closely-cropped hair was now nearly white, and the thin, bony structure of his face stood out more skull-like than ever. But there was no change in the spellbinding aura of wealth and tradition that hovered about his tall, spare figure like a protective mist. I felt my stomach crawl with the same old nameless dread—it was like a quick glimpse through the gates of Hell.

"Colonel Yamata!" My voice struggled with a mixture of emotions; astonishment won the honors.

He bowed his head slightly. "Ah, Mr. Sheridan." His tone was cynical, sneering, melodious. "You cannot imagine what pleasure it gives me to welcome you once again aboard my ship."

I rubbed the aching area over my ear. "I only wish your invitation had been delivered with more standard protocol." The words came automatically, while my mind struggled unsuccessfully to bring some logic to the situation.

His mask of a face betrayed a brief pained look. "I must apologize for the rudeness with which it was delivered—but my goodwill ambassador was instructed to be cautious. The last time we parted company, you will recall, was under rather strenuous circumstances."

"I apologize for the rudeness of my farewell."

His wooden face splintered in a sudden smile. "You give me the opportunity to be magnanimous. All is fair in love and war, Mr. Sheridan."

"And now that the war is over—?"

It was difficult to remain nonchalant under his long, searching scrutiny, but I was damned if I'd give him the satisfaction of knowing I was overawed—and somewhat apprehensive.

Finally, he spoke. "Mr. Sheridan, I am quite impressed. There appears to be a certain hardness about you, a self-containment, that I find very intriguing. I hope I have, in some small measure, been responsible for this masterful maturity."

I sighed heavily. We had complied with the oriental niceties long enough. "I can scarcely believe, Colonel, that the development of my character is the primary purpose of this command performance."

He leaned back in his chair, nodding agreeably. "Impulsive as ever. But—as ever—so right." His manicured fingers plucked a dark Egyptian cigarette from a heavy, chased-silver case. As he inhaled delicately, the cabin boy made a silent reappearance, balancing a frosted decanter and two glasses on an ivory inlaid tray. He placed it on the glass-topped table at Colonel Yamata's elbow and disappeared like a genie into his bottle. I noticed the chess pieces set up on the table for the first time.

After he had filled both the glasses and handed me one, he made a negligent gesture toward the chessmen.

"You have no idea, Mr. Sheridan, how deeply indebted I am to you for teaching me the complexities of the game. That an occidental should instruct an oriental has never ceased to be a source of wry amusement to me. And it has also taught me never to underestimate an opponent."

Since his comments called for no answer, I volunteered none, burying my face in the drink instead. It was a gin sling. The hair of a very good dog.

"One dislikes crass commercialism," he went on, "but have you any idea what those chess pieces might be worth?"

His opaque, almond eyes followed me as I leaned forward for a better look.

"Jade. Carved jade," I diagnosed. "Mounted on an ebony base. The opposing pieces are some sort of crystal."

"Yes. Rose quartz."

I sat back in my chair, wondering what he was leading up to. "Damned expensive, no doubt. Better than I could ever hope to own."

"They are priceless, Mr. Sheridan. They date back to the Sung dynasty of China … and they are yours."

I gave him a long, searching look but could read no meaning into his inscrutable expression. Having noted the arrangement of the chess problem he was working out, I automatically reached forward and slid a bishop across the red diagonal. "Check!"

He sat up with a small sigh and examined the move. As he pondered, he spoke offhandedly. "Of course, we are both aware that you are not so naive as to suppose you were brought aboard my ship without purpose..."

"A price tag, Colonel?"

Moving a knight, he blocked his king from check and sat back with a pleased smile.

"But it is such a small price tag compared with what I have to offer." He glanced about at the easy elegance of his white yacht, the polished brass rails, the clean sweep of its hull. After a moment of appreciation he turned back to give me an enigmatic look.

"A beautiful ship, Colonel," I agreed.

"You can have one just like it—and almost anything else you might want. You can indulge any hobby. Horses, travel, women—whatever you desire, it is yours."

As I listened, I sensed, with a vague, uneasy trepidation, the mounting excitement burning beneath his controlled exterior.

"Best of all, you will have freedom from the grubby, mind-dulling necessity of earning a living. You will have freedom to develop your spirit, your soul. You will have freedom to enjoy all the wonders of the world, the arts, the beauty of life..."

"Very persuasive, Colonel," I interrupted. "But whenever I get something for nothing it takes a doctor to cure me."

There was an unaccustomed flush to his high cheek bones and a hot glitter to his eyes, belying the casual voice.

"You disappoint me," he said. "Are not the rewards worthy of a supreme gamble—almost of life itself?" Leaning forward and tapping a tapered forefinger on the arm of his chair for emphasis, he continued in slow, measured tones. "Mr. Sheridan—on the bottom of Caballo Bay, just off Corregidor, still lies nearly fourteen million Philippine pesos. Seven million dollars' worth. It is to be had for the taking!"

In startled amazement I stared into his feverish face.

"But I thought the U.S. Navy had salvaged the treasure long ago."

"They tried; however, they attempted the job with inadequate equipment and brought up only a negligible quantity of silver. In 1946, when the Philippines were granted their independence, your government abandoned salvage operations."

I suspected the answer, but I asked anyway. "Why didn't the Filipinos go after it?"

He sat back with a sigh. "They did, Mr. Sheridan, they did. But they found absolutely nothing. The Americans had removed everything in sight. The main bulk of the treasure, literally tons of it, had completely and mysteriously vanished!"

I gave him a blank stare.

The parchment skin of his face tautened with irritation. His eyes bored into mine like deep-well augers. "No comment, Mr. Sheridan?"

"Well," I shrugged, "if it is your intention to salvage the silver, it would seem you're under a bit of a handicap if you don't even know where it is."

"I don't know, Mr. Sheridan—but *you* do!"

He gave me no opportunity to either confirm or deny his statement. Persuasively, his speech was clipped with cold calculation. "I have all the equipment that is necessary; a good ship, competent help, and the best diving gear that money can buy. It won't be like last time. There is no risk, whatsoever."

"But that money belongs to the Bank of Manila," I pointed out. "It seems to me they would take a dim view of any free-lance efforts that didn't enjoy official sanction." I was still a bit stunned that the treasure had not been recovered. We had hidden it, but quickly and very crudely.

"Official sanction," he sneered, dismissing it with a languid wave. "Once I have the silver aboard my ship, and have moved out into the China Sea, nothing will interest me less than the opinions of petty officials." He reached out for the silver decanter and refilled our glasses without losing his grip on the conversation. "Mr. Sheridan, I have plotted every move with the precision of a chess game, leaving no element to chance. I have waited with great patience. I am prepared for any eventuality. And now the fruit is ripe, Mr. Sheridan. Rich, succulent, tasty."

I shook my head. "No. Count me out, Colonel," I said levelly. "Not on past scores—they are over and done with. But if I were interested I would go to the Bank of Manila and arrange, in a dull, legal manner, for salvage rights—with my compensation based on the amount I recovered. *If* I were interested." I poured down the dilute dregs of my drink. "As things stand I have another job to do."

Colonel Yamata indulged in a tight, smug smile. "Buying pearls, Mr. Sheridan? Have you not suspected that your mission may contain an element of duplicity?"

"I don't follow you." I felt inadequate. In fact, downright stupid.

With a thin smile, he reached into the pocket of his pale-grey morning jacket and pulled out his clenched hand, holding it toward me. Automatically, I held out my hand and he dropped two gleaming pearls into my palm. One was black; the other white.

For a moment I stared at them, hypnotized, then quickly grubbed about in my own pocket. They were still there. The two pairs were perfectly matched.

"It's a trick," I muttered. Literally and figuratively, I was at sea. On ebb tide.

Again he gave me that grimace he used for a smile. "It is no trick. As I told you—I have been planning for years. This is the beginning of the end, Mr. Sheridan. You were contacted by Mr. Tessa solely to maneuver you aboard my ship to engage your very valuable services. It has been a long, but far from dull, game."

I felt a bit grim. "So you had Tessa killed!"

He shook his head indifferently. "I lost a few inconsequential pawns, yes. But kill Rudolph Tessa, no. He was quite useful, in his blundering way, and I regret losing him. His mission was merely to lure you here on the pretext of examining a quantity of pearls. Unfortunately, less subtle means had to be employed after his regrettable demise. I detest force, Mr. Sheridan," he concluded with a pained sigh.

I had to hand it to him. He was quite an actor.

"Then what's all this about 'The Barracuda'? He appears to be a pretty deadly fish—and also interested in the treasure of Caballo Bay." I reached out to the chessboard, taking the Colonel's knight with my rook. "Check."

He ignored the move, his cold eyes drilling me with a long, hard look.

"Mr. Sheridan," he finally said. "I was under the impression that I had netted 'The Barracuda.'"

It was the second inference, direct and otherwise, that I might be something other than what I represented myself to be. It was becoming unnerving.

"Look," I said irritably, "this is all preposterous. My boss—Julius Wharton—sent me out here. He knows nothing about the Philippine silver."

Colonel Yamata stretched out his long legs and frosted me with another smile. "Quite right," he said. "But have you ever wondered about the identity of Julius Wharton's superior—the owner of the Great Western Importing Company?"

It was a blow to the solar plexus. I sucked in my breath sharply as the truth finally dawned on me. The cunning of the web this man had spun so patiently defied belief.

"But why? Why me? There were several of us who knew where the silver was hidden."

His smile faded. "Your selection of the past tense is admirably correct. There *were* several. Unfortunately, there were various mishaps. You are the only one left, Mr. Sheridan. The only one."

I could feel my jaw muscles ache as I clenched my teeth. "Why you lousy bastard," I gritted.

Gently he lifted a hand as if placating an angry child. "Please. Do not leap to conclusions. Perhaps I could be held responsible for the death of one. Swede Anderson proved remarkably adamant to persuasion while in prison camp during the terminal days of the war. The others ..." he shrugged indifferently, "the fortunes of war. Except for Morgan, of course. You know his fate."

I did. And felt sick to my stomach all over again. Poor, crippled Morgan. He never had a chance. Slowly I rose to my feet, kicking my chair out of the way. I wanted to smash the sadistic smile off his smug face. He watched me like a cat playing with a squeaking mouse.

"Violence, Mr. Sheridan?" he taunted. "Good! It is the last refuge of the intellectually defeated." His smile widened by a millimeter. "However, before engaging in precipitate action, I would suggest you check your flank—you will meet an old friend."

Whirling about, I stared into the tunnel-like bore of a snub-nosed revolver. Big as it was, the gun was almost lost in the huge hand of a hairy, barrel-chested figure. With a moronic grin he watched me, swaying back and forth like a gorilla on absurdly short, widely-spread legs.

From behind me came the softly jeering voice of Colonel Yamata. "Yes. It is Takahito, ex-sergeant of the Japanese military police. He, too, has been looking forward to meeting you once again."

The words crowded through my throat, thick with anger and hate. "All right, Yamata. Tell your butcher he might as well shoot. He will, sooner or later, anyway. Even if I cooperated with you in your hijacking swindle, you'd double-cross me in the end."

"Please, Mr. Sheridan." His voice was mildly amused. "I would not think of applying such crude measures. Takahito is present only in a defensive position."

"Great," I snarled. "Then tell him to stand aside. I'm leaving."

I started for the ladder amidship. There was a small dinghy tied up at the foot of it, bobbing on the ocean swell. Putting one hand on the rail, I turned toward Colonel Yamata, who was watching me with narrowed eyes. I was about to give him a snappy Japanese salute of farewell but, to my surprise, he suddenly clapped his hands. I followed the direction of his eyes as he looked toward the hatchway leading to the cabins.

When she appeared beneath the awning, I froze in disbelieving shock. Slim, regally erect, she was more beautiful than even my vivid memories. She was wearing a red kimono richly ornamented with gold dragons. Luxuriant black hair fell in soft waves, framing a composed, calm face. Only her eyes were different—the sparkle I remembered so well was gone, replaced by blue-porcelain emptiness.

"Tulana!" My voice croaked out of control.

"Hello, Jim."

I swiveled my head as the Colonel spoke up. "You see, Mr. Sheridan—I have your queen."

I don't know what I was thinking about, or even what I was doing. Like the mainspring of a watch that had been wound too tightly, I broke out of control. With a maddened rush, I charged directly at Takahito, blindly indifferent to his gun. With a deft motion he whipped it high in the air and chopped down at my head.

As I dived for the bottom of the empty swimming pool again, I heard a strange phrase echo boomingly against the sides.

"Checkmate, Mr. Sheridan!"

CHAPTER FIVE

Manila in the spring will never offer Paris any serious competition, at least as far as beauty and the Left Bank are concerned. But in the year 1941, the economic advantages were keenly appreciated by impecunious students of Far Eastern cultures—in particular, one by the name of James B. Sheridan who had cashed in his dollars for pesos and had holed up in one of the more colorful hotels—the better to sample tropical romance.

I soon found it delightfully easy to become acquainted with the local flora and fauna, and particularly impossible not to become well-acquainted with the proprietor of the Casa Grande, Jacques Julian Costeau. He was of the type who lives life in capital letters, who enlarges every incident to Homeric proportions, who expands each casual friendship to V.I.P. stature. And because I was from the States, and because I was a student of culture, I was—ipso facto—an expert on all things bohemian; like jazz, booze and girls. My undenied talents were put to the test only once...

It was "The Sugar Blues" played like it hadn't been played since Clyde McCoy. Lifting my brows in surprise, I right-angled from my course across the tiled lobby and followed the sweet, melancholy strains into the casino. Costeau was his own, and only, customer. Seated on a bar stool with his back toward me, he was listening to the trumpet with his head propped against his fist. The bartender saw me coming and his hand automatically reached for a bottle of rum. I nodded and climbed onto the stool behind Costeau, listening until the music evaporated like the odor of sweet wine.

"My God!" I said softly. "Where did you find him?"

Startled, Costeau jerked around, then gave me a broad smile. "Ah, *mon ami!* Good, is he not?" He tugged at his drooping mustache in pleasure. "I think my customers they are getting tired of congas and tangos. I am trying to assemble a whole new evening of entertainment. Something new, something different."

"Sounds great," I said, "but he can't play 'The Sugar Blues' all evening. What else have you got?"

He gave a massive shrug and poured half a tumbler of gin down his cavernous throat.

"But that is my trouble," he complained, wiping his mouth. "So far I have only him. And, of course, the pianist."

"Of course," I grinned. Henry, the ebony pianist, owned a small piece of the Casa Grande.

A tall, cadaverous Filipino came out onto the small stage with a guitar and started his audition, unfortunately with a tango. Costeau gave him brief attention, then turned back to me.

"I need a star for the show. A—what you call it—a stellar attraction."

"I can play 'Home on the Range' on a Chinese flute."

He gulped more gin.

"How about Fatima?"

He looked at me suspiciously. "Who is this Fatima?"

"An Egyptian belly dancer down at the Tripoli."

"*Sacré!* You are in a droll mood."

"And you're hypercritical. Let's see. How about Nghia Lao?"

This time he didn't bother to answer. Just glared at me.

"One of those Cambodian neck jerkers," I explained, giving him what I thought was a superb illustration. "And a real cute trick."

He sighed heavily. "I am beginning to think *your* neck should be jerked. You do not appreciate the gravity of my situation."

He glanced back toward the piano where a girl stood, hesitantly speaking to Henry. The pianist was leaning forward to catch the softly spoken words. A wild tangle of hair dropped like a black waterfall to her shoulders. Her dress was a cheap cotton print worn in the loose, baggy native style. Under the baby spotlight her face was bleached and plain without make-up.

Costeau groaned. "And who is this?" he asked the bartender.

"I don't know," he said, "but I'll go find out for you."

"It's Tulana," I interposed. "She sings at the Bomba."

"The Bomba!" he echoed. "Thirty years I've lived in Manila and I've never heard of the Bomba. You've been here one year—you know the Bomba. Where is it?"

"A dump down on the waterfront. Tough and dirty."

He gave me a speculative look. "For a student archaeologist you are to be found in some very strange places."

I toasted him with my drink. "Never know where I'll dig up something good. Take Tulana there, for instance. Her singing will curl your toes."

As I finished speaking, Henry ran his fingers down the keys in an introductory passage, then moved softly as cats' feet into the chords of a song I didn't recognize. Tulana faced us and began to sing.

Her voice wasn't particularly good. Too husky. Too low. But somehow she poured out a native song of the mountains and dark forests and sparkling seas with a haunting vibrancy that gripped you like a magnet. I could see the spell working itself on Costeau, who was staring at her with his mouth partly open.

The last note softly died and she simply stood there, waiting. Costeau looked down at his shoes, then back at me. "My toes didn't curl."

"I forgot to tell you—you're supposed to listen to Tulana with your shoes off."

"I sometimes don't think you've got a serious bone in your head."

Nevertheless, he turned back to the girl and called out to her to sing another number. I could feel the bewilderment in his voice. He couldn't figure out why he wanted to hear her again, but he did. Like I said, it was magnetic. After that number, he had her go through two more. Finally he beckoned to her to join us.

She approached, dark-blue eyes skittering back and forth between us, frightened, hopeful. Her features were smooth and regular, at least. Which, come to think of it, was more than I could say for my own.

Costeau reached out behind her. Her eyes followed his arm like it was a hairy snake.

"Don't be frightened, child," he said. "But we'd like to know if there's anything in this tent you are wearing."

He grasped her dress, snugging it up closely to her body in front. There was something in it, all right. I could feel my toes curl.

"Eh?" he said, trying to get a look from the front at the same time he was wadding up the dress in back. "Do you think we can make something of her?"

"Well, if you can't—I can."

"Damn it, be serious."

I sighed. "Jacques, *mon vieux*. It will be difficult. She is just a peasant girl, uneducated and simple. She can sing, but she knows none of the little tricks, the mannerisms. She has no poise. I'll bet she can't even write her own name. Haven't you got anything else?"

"But no," he almost cried. "And I must have a singer for tonight."

"I'm beginning to appreciate the gravity of your situation," I grinned, sliding off my stool. "Let me know how you make out."

Before I could make my escape, he grabbed me by the arm and, in five minutes, fast-talked me into taking her down to a department store and buying her an evening gown so she would look presentable for the evening.

"Just one," he said. "Perhaps I can find a replacement for tomorrow night. Charge it to my account."

"Where else?" I muttered. I turned toward Tulana, who had remained silent and big-eyed throughout the entire conversation, and switched back to Spanish. "Come, *mucha-cha*, let us go shopping."

I hustled her out through the lobby and into a cab, where she examined the interior with interest before settling back tentatively against the cushions next to me. I got the distinct impression this was her first ride in an automobile. We rode in complete silence for fifteen minutes before she spoke, her eyes straight ahead.

"I, too, onderstand the English," she said.

I gave her a quick, jolted look, immediately recalling my callous conversation with Costeau. My face began to burn. I could have melted and run down through the cracks in the floorboards.

"Oh," I said, brightly.

Five more minutes in silence. I looked at her from the corner of my eye.

"Where did you get a name like Tulana?" I asked.

No answer.

"It's Polynesian. Are you part Polynesian?"

More silence.

"And dark-blue eyes and a wide forehead. That's Nordic. Denmark?"

The silence got silenter.

"Two parts Spanish. One part Danish. One part Polynesian. Right?"

I never did find out.

I found the ladies' dress salon in the department store and led Tulana up to a pleasant, white-haired lady who appeared to be in charge. After explaining what I wanted, I withdrew to perch uncomfortably on a stiff, two-passenger couch and watch the goings on.

Tulana came to life, chattering with bright animation as they rummaged through rack after rack of dresses. After endless consultation, she narrowed the choice down to five or six gowns. I had to hand it to her. She had marvelous instinct. The smiling saleslady suggested she take them all into the fitting room and try each one on. I approved.

"And," she went on, lifting her fine white brows questioningly, "may I take her in to the coiffeur and fix her hair? It won't take too long."

"Pray do," I agreed, fervently.

Time dragged by. The couch petrified beneath me. Several pretty girls whirled in, smiling as they went by. Ever the gentleman, I smiled back. They held dresses up for each other to examine, then glanced sidelong at me. Sometimes I shook my head. Sometimes I nodded. But I couldn't see that it made any difference in what they selected.

A girl came out from behind a curtain, dressed in a blue gown of curve-hugging design. Colored sequins sparkled in appropriate places. Glistening black hair, done up in tight ringlets, cascaded down the nape of her slender neck. She walked by me with an erect, haughty stride, a remote smile on her beautiful face. I swiveled my neck, gaping like a peasant in the big city. A voice came from in front of me.

I unwound my neck. "What?" I asked, blankly. The saleslady was smiling at me. "Say!" I expostulated, looking at my watch. "I've been here an hour and a half. How much longer is this rebuilding job going to take?"

"But it is done, señor." Her eyes followed the girl in blue as she came around the other side of my couch.

I looked again. "Well, I'll be damned," I breathed in awe.

With reckless enthusiasm I told the saleslady to wrap up all of the evening gowns, with a couple of street dresses for good measure. Tulana disappeared again and came out a few minutes later dressed in a soft, gray suit. It was wonderful what she could do to clothes.

The saleslady handed me a pile of packages. "I am certain you have made your wife very happy, *señor*," she said.

"What? Oh. Yes. Me, too."

When we had settled in a cab for the return trip to the Casa Grande, Tulana turned to me with fire in her eye.

"Why did you tell that lady I was your wife?" she demanded.

"Me? I didn't. All I said was 'yes'."

"It was the same thing."

"Well, what else could I say—that I didn't know you, but I enjoyed buying dresses for lovely young ladies?"

Suddenly her cheeks dimpled and her face was transformed in a smile. It was like watching the sun come up.

"I think you are really very nice, very wonderful," she said softly.

She got no argument from me. I just hoped Costeau was as good at character analysis. I had just spent two hundred of his dollars.

Tulana was an immediate, stunning, fantastic success. Within a few weeks there was standing-room only in the casino of Casa Grande. Costeau's smile was so broad that his swinging mustaches were permanently two inches further apart.

I was always there in the evening when it came time for her to sing, listening to the crowd hush expectantly as she smiled into the changing colors of the spotlight and started to sing in her husky, compelling voice. I didn't dare take my shoes off. I would never have gotten them back on. Somehow I had the conceit to think she was singing only to me.

We began to enjoy the late afternoons together. After my classes at the University, we would drive up into the mountains on a picnic or go swimming at remote beaches. But she always managed to keep me at arm's length. And she would only go with me in the afternoons. Never in the evening. Every day, precisely at six o'clock, she would mysteriously disappear, to appear again at the casino just before ten when it was time for her first number. I grew stupidly jealous of these secret missions, but could never learn their purpose. Finally, one afternoon on the patio, I decided to bring it to a head, insisting we spend an evening together.

"Please, Jim," she said, "please don't ask me. Not yet."

I exploded with pent-up anger. "Then, damn it, tell me where you go every evening."

She turned away, shaking her head. "I can't. Perhaps I will some day. But I can't tell you now."

I grabbed her by the shoulders and turned her back roughly. "Have you got a lover? Is that it? Or are you married? Do you go home to the waiting husband every day?"

She jerked away from my grasp, covering her face with her hands. "No. No," she choked. "Please. Leave me alone." With a convulsive sob, she ran through the archway, leaving me standing frustrated and fatheaded.

I behaved like a child. Leaving her strictly alone, I began playing the field again. But it worked both ways. Whenever I made a late, surreptitious entrance into the casino to hear her sing, I always found a covey of admiring males surrounding her. So I stayed further away than ever.

Heavy, ominous rumblings were coming from the north as the Japanese started rattling sabers and dancing to the beat of war drums. I enlisted in the Air Corps. Based on interminable tests and my R.O.T.C experience in the University, they slapped a couple of gold lieutenant bars on my shoulders and assigned me to the intelligence section to do code work. I was to report to Henderson Field the following day.

Late that night I got back to the Casa Grande. I went into the casino to find Jacques Costeau and buy him a farewell drink. We hadn't talked with each other for quite some time—since my argument with Tulana, in fact.

The casino was crowded as usual, but I found the big Frenchman at a sheltered corner of the bar. He lifted his beetling brows at the sight of my uniform and gave my hand a hard clasp.

"Ahh," he shook his head sadly. "So it has come to this, eh?"

I nodded, sneaking a quick glance toward the stage. The cadaverous guitar player was strumming a tango. Jacques had hired him because he looked so "hongry."

"I'm afraid so," I answered. "I'm betting the roof blows off before long."

"But it will not last long, my friend. We will stuff them down Fujiyama and put the lid back on." He ordered two drinks, full of fight. "They are not soldiers, these Japs, they are nothing but gardeners."

I gave him a tired smile. "Well, here's hoping they don't decide to plant their crops in the Philippines."

The guitar player finished to mild applause. A small combo of negroes wearing red fezzes came out with a blare of trumpets. I looked at my watch.

Costeau watched me with a knowing smile. "She will be on next," he said quietly. He pushed my drink toward me. "It is none of my business, old one, but I have often wondered what happened."

I chucked down part of my Rum Sour. "I don't know. Tell me—I'm stupid. It started out with a little argument, then got so big that neither of us could handle it."

"Argument? About what? Punch me in the nose if you wish."

I shrugged. "About nothing. About where she went every day from six until ten in the evening. About my prying idiocy."

Slowly he straightened up and looked at me strangely. "That's what it was about? Only that?"

"Yeah. Only that."

His eyes grew heavy and he let out a deep breath. "She is a very proud girl, my friend, proud as only those of Spanish blood can be—blind, stiff-necked proud. She *couldn't* tell you."

I set my glass on the bar slowly and stared at him. "You mean you know?"

"Of course. She told me. Next to you, she felt like a stupid little peasant girl, barefoot from the mountains. Unworthy of the brilliant James Sheridan. So she is taking night courses at school. English, dramatics, literature, everything. From six to ten every day, and private tutors on weekends. You clumsy fool, she is in love with you!"

I slumped down on my stool as I listened. "My God," I said when he had finished, "I haven't done a thing right since I first met her." I felt as empty as a robbed cash register.

She came onstage in a pink evening gown that was both simple and chic, revealing and concealing. I sucked in my breath sharply, realizing how beautifully poised she had become, how she held the audience in the palm of her hand—and me along with it. She started to sing, her eyes sweeping the crowded casino, lingering here and there on enthralled, listening faces. She looked past me as though I were invisible.

The song died to the roar of clapping hands and shouts that made the chandeliers sway. Abruptly she whirled and disappeared behind the velvet curtain.

I got up, making some excuse to Costeau, and went up to my room. Without turning on the lights, I entered and crossed over to the wood-slatted doors and flung them open. Brief gusts of rain were rustling the bushes in the courtyard below, twisting the spray from the fountain. I lit a cigarette and leaned against the railing. Heavy drops began to splot loudly on the tiles with the measured monotony of a metronome. I smoked the cigarette down to my fingernails, then flipped it toward the pool. It missed.

Closing the doors against the rain, I undressed and lay down. Sleep was as elusive as tomorrow's hopes, but finally the dreams came, wild and distorted, with distant, booming cannon and olive-gray trucks racing in the wrong direction. Suddenly a crash jerked me upright in bed and I saw a flash of lightning fade away. Before it disappeared I caught a glimpse of a figure silhouetted against the open door, fully and beautifully curved under a semi-transparent negligee.

"Jim!" she cried. "Jacques told me. You are going away!"

Her English was wonderful. So was she.

CHAPTER SIX

And, then, the war was upon us. Not with the blare of trumpets and crashing Wagnerian overtures—but with bewilderment and fatigue, confusion and hopelessness, with overpowering, seemingly invincible little men in jungle-green uniforms that popped from the trees, snaked through the brush, slithered across the swamps. Always we retreated as we fought desperate rear-guard actions. First we fell back toward Manila, then toward the bay, then northward in a frantic race to gain the north end of Bataan peninsula before we were cut off by the ubiquitous little green men. Most of us made it—a motley, ragtail army with its back to the sea, headed for the stunning, disbelieving chaos of surrender.

A few of us managed to prolong the agony by crossing the few miles of water that separated the lower end of the peninsula from the "impregnable" fortress of Corregidor. Once there we had just enough time to take a deep breath, grab something to eat, and report for duty again.

My first assignment was to take command of a series of gun emplacements along the east ridge. I managed to zigzag my way up the steep slope through a murderous barrage of shellfire, when suddenly a big one nearly dropped in my back pocket.

Groaning, I sat up as loose dirt spilled off my back and rattled tinnily down onto my helmet. I reached around mechanically, dumped the dirt out of it, and replaced it on my head. Then I looked up at the sober face of the corporal, who was kneeling next to me in the gun emplacement. He grinned with relief.

"Where am I?" I winced groggily and gingerly probed at my shoulder.

His grin widened. "You're in the biggest goddamn foxhole on Corregidor, Lieutenant. And you're here only to protect the interests of the American warmongers, the oil companies, and the munitions industry. I know because I just heard Tokyo Rose explain everything to us poor, misguided G.I.'s the other night on the radio." He changed the subject abruptly. "Howdaya feel, Lieutenant?"

"Ready for cremation," I muttered. "And somebody must have ripped off my arm, then stuck it back on wrong—it hurts like hell."

He shook his head with an admiring look. "I ain't surprised. I never seen such a dandy dive like you made when that shell started whistling. You musta come fifteen feet through the air. Didn't know if you were landing dead or alive."

I rubbed the bruised muscles of my shoulder. "I'm still not sure."

We hit the dirt again as another shell landed a few yards away, higher up the ridge. A cloud of dust eddied down into our excavation. The tired, red-rimmed eyes of the corporal watered as he was seized in a convulsive coughing spell that strained the chords of his thin neck. The next shell missed our ridge completely, screaming in its angry trajectory from Bataan to Malinta Hill behind us.

I got up and went over to the five-inch field gun that poked its snout through the sand bags. It looked like something left behind by Magellan.

"Does this relic really work?"

"Yes, sir," he choked. "Works fine—if you're aimin' at China."

He was right. It was mounted in a fixed position to guard the north entrance to Manila Bay. But the Japs were uncooperative, having taken the land route by sweeping down through Bataan.

The gun was as useless as a cap pistol. I turned back to the corporal with a sigh. I wasn't much of a cannon-shooter, anyway.

"What's your name?" I asked.

"Joe Price. Corporal Joe Price, sir." He tried to wipe the dirt off his face with the torn sleeve of his shirt, but only succeeded in rearranging it over a wider area. His face was young-old with exhaustion; his mouse-brown hair sadly in need of shearing.

"Why don't you come up here, out of that dust cloud, before you choke to death?" I suggested.

He shook his head firmly. "No thank you. When I got here this morning, the burial detail was picking up pieces of the last gun crew. I don't need fresh air that bad."

It struck me as a bit of good logic so I didn't press the point. Cautiously, I peered over the top of the sand bags toward the green mass of Bataan. Except for a few puffs of swirling smoke rising above the trees on the peninsula, there was nothing unusual to be seen—just the pale blue sky, and the sea, calm as molten lava beneath the hot, tropical sun. It was hard to believe that death crawled toward us, implacably and irresistibly, under the dense cover of the jungle like fleas on a dog's back.

I turned back to Joe, who was sitting with his thin arms clasped about his legs and staring into the dirt.

"They didn't expect you to man this gun by yourself, did they?"

"Cripes, I hope not! I was a tank driver—with the 192nd Tank Battalion."

"We make a great team," I said. "I am, or was, attached to the 93rd Squadron."

"Jeez. A pilot?"

"No. Communications. Right now I'm supposed to keep checking six of these gun emplacements to make sure you guys don't run out of ammunition."

He snorted. "The only thing I've had a chance to run out of is cigarettes."

I grinned and tossed him my pack. "Keep them. I'll bring you some more on my next trip around."

He caught them in mid-air, thanking me profusely as he stabbed one into his mouth and lit it. Leaning back on one elbow he exhaled with a great, satisfied sigh and returned my grin. And somehow the atmosphere suddenly changed from that of lieutenant and corporal to just two tired guys in a foxhole.

"When did you come over here to Corregidor?" I asked him.

"Yesterday afternoon. My tank got hit two days ago. I was the only one that didn't get killed—didn't even get a scratch. The Japs came up and looked inside, but I pretended to be dead and they went away. I laid there all afternoon with the tank commander staring at me. That was bad enough—but then the flies started swarming in, crawling over his face. God! I kept remembering I owed him five bucks he loaned me on our last night in Manila."

He stopped for a moment, his face set in tired, grim lines, then went on: "When it got dark I crawled out and hit for the jungle and started walking south. When it got daylight I found I was right near the road to Mariveles. I could hear trucks. I went over to the road and found it was jammed with equipment and columns of infantry. Some of the trucks had white pieces of cloth tied on them. I asked a guy what they were for—it didn't dawn on me they were surrender flags. Some captain told me to go with them to a clearing where we were supposed to pile up our weapons. I decided to hell with that business—I wasn't handing over my rifle to no Japs. They had to come and take it away from me. I kept walking south until I got to Mariveles. When I got there I found a bunch of guys—marines, army, air force—grabbing everything that would float and heading for Corregidor. I got on one of the fishing boats and came over. So here I am."

I nodded. It was a familiar story. I had gotten to Mariveles too late for the luxury of a boat trip and, under cover of darkness, swam the two or three miles separating Bataan from Corregidor.

Someone brought the small matter of sharks to my attention after I had crawled up on the rocky shore.

Joe spoke up as he offered me one of my cigarettes with a magnanimous gesture.

"Lieutenant, do you think we'll be able to hold out here until help comes?"

I looked at him blankly. "Until help comes?"

"Yeah. I heard this morning that a relief squadron of ships was coming up from Australia."

I shook my head, pretending to think it over. Apparently he didn't know that MacArthur was headed in the other direction with a squadron of PT boats. For all his youth, Joe was a scrappy little fighter—and all he had left was a pathetic bit of hope.

"Damned if I know, Joe. A submarine came in this morning with a load of ammunition and medicine. They're unloading it now."

"Jeez, I sure wish …" He broke off in mid-sentence and stared over my head.

I craned my neck around and found Captain Tyler peering over the top of the sand bags. His fat face was covered with a muddy gray mask of sweat and dust.

"Hey, Sheridan," he said. "The Major wants you down at the dock. Pronto. I'm supposed to take over for you."

I nodded, not bothering to ask what it was all about. Tyler was the kind who wouldn't have known anyway. He was the "ours not to reason why" type. Halfway up the embankment I paused and turned to Joe.

"Don't fire until you see the whites of their eyes," I said.

He gave me a tired half-salute. "O.K., Lieutenant, but that ain't what I'm gonna aim at."

I scrambled up the high ridge that formed part of Corregidor's protective backbone and dropped into comparative safety on the south side. By now, however, the heavy shelling in our area had ceased, the Japs having moved their bombardment pattern toward the eastern end of the island. I followed the narrow gauge railroad which had been dive-bombed so often that from the air it must have looked like a long series of dots and dashes. At the dots, which were deep bomb craters, the rails were twisted into weird pretzel shapes.

When I got to the road I found it in no better shape than the railroad. Several smoke-blackened skeletons of trucks, some with gun carriages behind them, were lying in the ditches. A few of the trucks appeared undamaged, probably either out of gas or abandoned by their drivers, who had suddenly found they had compelling business elsewhere. Further down the hill I could see that the airfield runway was useless, having received the most concentrated efforts of Japanese bombs and shellfire. One of the hangars was a blazing red inferno, a black column of smoke twisting lazily above it into the blue sky. No one seemed to pay any attention to it.

I picked my way through the debris of what had once been the barracks area, feeling better when I finally got within the shadow of Malinta Hill's looming hulk. The damage here was considerably less—and the population of Corregidor's defenders increased in direct proportion. Everywhere, with the same haggard expressions, were soldiers, sailors, marines, civilians. They wandered about with aimless lack of direction, trying to find someone in authority to tell them what to do.

The medical corps didn't have to be told. Ambulances and littermen with their heavy burdens moved toward the tunnel in a never-ending stream.

The dock area was congested: packing cases of food and supplies stacked up in mountainous piles, trucks creeping hesitantly through the littered streets, tired men everywhere, sullenly silent or irritably bellicose.

Major Russo was easy to find in spite of the confusion. I could hear his voice booming like a foghorn from one of the docks. As I made my way toward him, I saw the sleek black hull of a submarine tied up alongside. A couple of navy officers were standing on the deck, grinning at the scene on the dock below them.

Major Russo was standing with his back toward me as he bellowed mightily at a work crew of Filipino civilians. They were staring at the sub, not paying him the slightest bit of attention. I tapped him on the shoulder.

"Heard you wanted me, Major," I said. "What's .up?"

He whirled around, his bulldog face red with exasperation.

"Oh, Sheridan," he nearly smiled with relief. "You're just in time. I was ready to shoot the whole goddamned bunch of them. I heard you could speak Spanish?"

I nodded.

"Then please take this blankety blank gang up to the tunnel. Report to General LaVine. Tell him you have the crew that's to load the gold."

"Load the gold," I echoed blankly. "What the hell are we going to do—bribe General Homma?"

He shook his head in irritation. "All the gold, silver, and valuable papers from the Bank of Manila has been brought over so the Japs won't get it. We've taken the ammo off this pigboat— now we're to put the gold back into it for ballast. It's going to the States."

"Can't they ballast it with men?"

He gave a sardonic laugh. "Since when are men worth more than money?"

Malinta Tunnel was seething with activity, which appeared confused and aimless. After several pieces of misinformation I finally found my way to the High Command area.

It was harder than cracking a bank vault, but I finally managed to bulldoze my way past the guards that covered the doors leading to the inner sanctum of General LaVine. My last roadblock was a stiff-necked character with a stiff black mustache. The little sign on his desk said he was a colonel by the name of J. J. Montrose.

"Major Russo sent me," I explained, "to report to General LaVine." I gave him a stiff salute.

He lifted an indifferent eyebrow. "Do you have a name?"

A real cutie.

"Lieutenant James B. Sheridan, 93rd Squadron, serial number ..."

"You can't see him," cutie interrupted. "He's in conference."

"But I'm supposed to ..."

"A very important conference. Come back later."

I shrugged. "O.K. by me, Colonel. I've got a dandy little war going outside that'll keep me busy for a while. But I understand General LaVine has some gold we're supposed to put on a submarine ..."

He sighed and stood up with drooping shoulders. "Well, why didn't you say so in the first place?" He jerked his head, meaning for me to follow him, and went over to the door behind his desk. Opening it, he got me inside with another jerk.

As I stepped into the conference room, a few heads turned my way briefly and I could see the harassed, beaten look in their eyes. Although they returned immediately to the litter of maps and papers on the long table, my one quick glimpse told me what I had feared. I could even feel it. The surrender of Corregidor was only a matter of hours away.

Numbly, I waited near the door as Colonel Montrose went over to the conference table and spoke to a deep-chested soldier with a crewcut. The soldier looked toward me, nodded, and got up. I saw the small gold star on each shoulder as he approached. His shirt was open at the throat and his sleeves rolled up as high as they would go.

This time I was prepared to identify myself but apparently he didn't give a damn who I was. He gave me a quick rundown in a deep, staccato voice while his gray eyes measured me for size.

"In one of the storage tunnels—Colonel Montrose will show you where—is nearly eighteen million dollars in gold and silver bullion. Also valuable papers. Have your crew load the gold and papers on the submarine. All of the silver is to be loaded aboard a scow. Check with Major Russo on that—he knows which one. Watch your men so they don't try to load up their own pockets."

He eyed me closely, but didn't insult me by adding any more. Abruptly he turned away and rejoined the officers at the table, where he continued his conversation as though nothing could interest him less than eighteen million dollars. Colonel Montrose's eyes jerked me out of the room.

There were four guards with submachine guns protecting the entrance to the storage chamber, two inside and two outside. Colonel Montrose gave them new orders, putting them under my command temporarily, and then departed after giving me a stiff look. I suspect he figured it was the last time he'd ever see either me or the gold.

Somehow I had the idea this was going to be a simple little chore that we could knock off in a few hours but, to my amazement, I found the room jammed with row after row of heavy wooden boxes. I whistled and turned to the nearest guard.

"My God! How many boxes are there in this pile?"

He settled his horn-rimmed glasses and gave me a steely look. "One thousand seven hundred and thirty, sir. Each weighs approximately three hundred pounds, or two hundred fifty-nine and a half tons. The boxes of silver each contain six thousand pesos, worth three thousand American dollars. The gold boxes ..."

I held up my hand. "O.K., O.K. You must have been on guard duty here for some time."

Grimly, he looked straight ahead at the pile of boxes. "Ever since they brought the goddamned stuff over from Manila, sir."

I clucked sympathetically. "Helluva way to fight a war, eh?"

"Yes, sir. You said it, sir."

To show him what the outside world looked like, I took him and the other inside guard along with us to protect our struggling little convoy as the men lugged the heavy boxes—two men to a box—out into the tunnel, loaded them into jeeps, and took them down to the docks. There they were loaded by navy men into the submarine. The guards were only window dressing. No one paid any attention to us except an army nurse who glanced at the stenciled markings on the boxes, gave me a sweet smile and chanted: "Fifteen men on a dead man's chest, yo ho ho…" I grinned back. I thought it was funny…at the time.

At midnight I took a break with Major Russo. He uncorked a thermos jug of coffee, poured it into the cups, laced it with a bit of private stock from a small flask, and then held up his cup.

"To the end of the war—for us," he said grimly.

It was a bitter toast.

"So it's true?" I asked. "I've been hearing the rumor all day. Do you know when?"

He shrugged. "Tomorrow. Next day, maybe. That's why we're trying to get this job done tonight while it's still dark." He looked out toward the dark sheet of water that reflected the blackness of night. "Caballo Bay is protected by the high ridge of Corregidor from any direct observation by the Japs on Bataan. If they knew what we were up to they would be plastering every square inch of the bay."

I stared at him. "You mean all this silver we're loading on the scow is to be dumped into Caballo Bay?"

"Right. There's no place else to go with it. We certainly don't want the Japs to get it. So we're taking it out about two miles and dumping it into a hundred feet of water. They'll probably find out about it, but they'll have a helluva time getting their hands on it."

I sounded more optimistic than I felt. "Maybe we'll be back before they can bring it up."

He shook his head heavily. "I wish I could believe that. But it's going to be a long, hard comeback. We're even dumping a lot of the stuff the submarine brought in, along with rifles, ammunition, torpedoes, spare parts. I guess this is the end of the line for us in this war."

CHAPTER SEVEN

At first the Jap troops were wildly elated. Like their most beautiful opium dreams had come true. And they never missed a chance to rub in the fact that they had broken mighty America's power in the Far East.

But it was no rougher than we had expected. In their steady advance across Luzon, then down the peninsula of Bataan, they had outrun their own supply lines and things were a bit chaotic. While they were getting reorganized, we were allowed comparative freedom of the island during the daylight hours and we put this to use, trying to find food while we were out on work details. Feeding their prisoners was an effort the Japs considered unnecessary to the furtherance of the war.

I volunteered for every detail that came along. It made the time pass faster. Also, being able to understand Japanese, I could learn quite a bit about what was going on. And I constantly kept my eyes open for any opportunity to escape.

As the days went by our numbers reduced rapidly. The Japs were sending everyone who wasn't needed for their dirty work to the prison camp at Cabanatuan. Some were sent directly to Japan. As our numbers continued to dwindle, I occasionally wondered what quirk of fate still kept me on the island. I found out in the hot dawn of another blistering, tropical day. One of the guards stood next to me after waking me up by kicking the bottom of my bunk.

"You come," he rasped. "General Tonoya wants to see you."

General Tonoya was looking out the window toward the placid surface of Caballo Bay. A soft offshore breeze rippled the water and it sparkled under the hot sun like shivered fragments of glass. Apparently absorbed in the beauty of it all, he let me admire his massive shoulder muscles that bulged under a short-sleeved shirt. His head was smooth-shaven, with a small roll of fat draped just below his ears. It almost hid his thick, stubby neck. Finally he turned toward us, his black eyes falling on the guard.

"Tell Hanusa I want him," he said. "Then you wait in the corridor." His voice was surprisingly soft and melodious on the surface, but there was a layer of steely authority beneath. A thin line of mustache on his lip made him look more English than Japanese. Except for his eyes—heavy-lidded, deep black pools that neither gave, nor expected, quarter. They regarded me with emotionless speculation.

"You have been treated quite well, Lieutenant Sheridan?" He spoke in Japanese.

I raised my eyebrows and stared at him as though I didn't understand.

He waited a moment, then sighed and went over to a desk cluttered with piles of manila folders. Seating himself, he opened one of the folders and read from it—in English.

"Lieutenant James B. Sheridan ... twenty-five years old ... six feet one inch tall ... black hair ... brown eyes ... speaks English, Spanish, French, Italian ... also Chinese, Japanese, several dialects ... has crescent-shaped scar on left thigh." He paused and looked up at me. "From what, may I ask?"

"I was bitten by an Imperial Dragon."

He nodded. "I hope your sense of humor stays with you."

I heard the door open behind me. I turned my head and saw a huge, ape-like figure waddle in on short, bandy legs. His face was as empty of intelligent expression as a headhunter's trophy. Coarse black hair hung down over his ears. Suppressing an involuntary shudder, I turned back to General Tonoya.

"My secretary." His eyes glinted with amusement. "He will take notes."

"With a baseball bat?"

"He carries that everywhere. He loves to play ball." He closed up the folder and leaned back in his chair. "And I hope that you, too, will play ball, Lieutenant—it makes for a much better game."

"Then let's see the pitch, General."

He clasped his hands behind his head and surveyed me with mild indulgence. Like a businessman about to tell an employee he would give him a raise—when business got a little better.

"I am quite pleased with you," he reassured me. "I don't think you are a fool. Certainly you have viewed the invincible power of Japan at close enough range to realize the war will soon be over, that the United States will never again interfere with our glorious destiny."

"Of course."

He gleamed with much happiness. "We are a determined race, Lieutenant, but a merciful one. Our hearts expand with our victories. For those who accept the inevitable graciously—even occidentals—we are prepared to make life very pleasant."

I made no comment. Two pitches gone by. At this point I preferred to look them over.

He unclasped his hands and leaned forward, keeping his eyes on mine. "Now, certain records have come to our attention which indicate that an enormous amount of silver and gold has been transferred to Corregidor from the Bank of Manila. It was stored in Malinta Tunnel. You know about that?"

"Yes."

He smiled happily. I had swung at a pitch.

"Where is it now?"

"Headed for the United States. It was loaded aboard a submarine the day before the surrender."

His smile dissolved abruptly and he shook his head in sharp irritation. "That is not true, Lieutenant. It is a statistical impossibility. A simple calculation has proved that there was nearly two hundred and fifty tons of treasure. That is far, far more than a submarine could accommodate under the circumstances. Now I repeat—where is it?"

I shrugged. "I don't know, General."

He compressed his lips until his mouth was just a thin slit. I could see his knuckles turn white as he gripped the arms of his chair. His voice was no longer melodious. It was as pleasant as a wood file that had suddenly hit a nail.

"Lieutenant Sheridan, I hope you do not prove me wrong by proving you *are* a fool. There is nothing to be gained by stupid stubbornness. Eventually we will find out anyway. Where is it?"

"I don't know."

He relaxed and slumped back with a hopeless shake of his head. His voice was soft again.

"Do not misunderstand me, Lieutenant. I am very patient. I have already accumulated a great deal of information. A barge was loaded with all of the silver and pulled out somewhere in the bay. A very small crew of Filipinos dumped the boxes overboard. They all apparently have died since then of various diseases. Only two officers were present, you and Major Russo."

It was my turn to grit my teeth. "Then why don't you ask Major Russo?" I had heard the Major died of a beating several days before.

For a long moment he simply stared at me, tapping a thick forefinger on the arm of his chair with monotonous regularity. Then his eyes slid past me, toward the wall at my rear.

"Hanusa," he said quietly. "I think we had better teach the Lieutenant how to play ball."

I had forgotten about the ape. I started to turn, but never made it. The bat hit me across my upper back like a runaway freight car, pitching me forward into the side of the desk. I groaned as I hit the floor. It felt like every bone in my back was broken. I took a few deep breaths and pulled myself up.

Through a dizzy haze of pain I could see that General Tonoya had neither moved nor changed expression. Then he smiled.

"Only the first inning, Lieutenant," he announced. "But perhaps you get the idea. Now—would you care to tell me where it is?"

The words ripped out, like stitches from an unhealed wound. "I can't tell you I don't know."

Hanusa moved me back from the desk with a crushing blow aimed at my chest. I threw up my arms to ward off the bat, but couldn't step back fast enough. I went down on my back. My arms had as much feeling as two socks stuffed with rags.

It went on. I tried to reach Hanusa but he swirled about in a foggy red mist. A soft, melodious voice occasionally worried about me. I told the voice I was a baseball. I fooled him—I was a seared, sick, squashed jellyfish. Finally I blacked out as though I had been dumped into a sea of Novocain.

I don't know where they kept me. In a room. In outer space. In an atom-splitter. But, even though I tried to hide behind a black wall of unconsciousness, they always found me and brought me back. With water. With ammonia. With oxygen.

Days went by. Blobs of agony strung on threads of fire.

"Where is it?"

"I don't know."

"Where is it?"

"I told you—I don't know."

"Where is it?"

"Dunno—dunno—dunno. Tol' ya, dunno."

Finally, a thousand years later, someone washed me off with a hose. Pushed me down a hundred miles of corridor. Propped me up in front of my friend, the General. He smiled.

"You're a lousy ballplayer, Lieutenant. We have found one of the Filipino workers who helped with the silver. He was a fine player—after we let him see you."

I tried to return his nice smile, but my face was an old leather boot.

"But it amuses me to keep you on the team," he went on. "Since you have such linguistic ability, you will be transferred to the salvage operation under the command of Colonel Yamata. You will assist by translating his orders into English."

"English!" I echoed hoarsely.

"Precisely. Six of your countrymen—all navy divers captured at Cavite—are more than anxious to cooperate."

I didn't believe it.

CHAPTER EIGHT

At least they decided that my battered hulk was worth saving. Carting me up to the hospital, they embalmed me with morphine, mummified me with gauze, and hung me up on pulleys so I'd be the right length and shape when I grew back together.

Three months and six quarts of plasma later, I was bounced from my private suite and convoyed by a guard from the hospital to North Dock. Sore because we had to walk, he dog-trotted most of the way and continually barked at me for lagging behind. With one arm still in the sling, and the other clutching a barracks bag of worldly goods, I found it impossible to keep pace. Besides, I didn't feel like it. I was sore, too.

There was a wooden guard shack set up at the land end of Pier 3. It was open on all sides like a hotdog stand at an amusement park, and had a flimsy tin roof that did no more than keep its two occupants from sunstroke. They laughed at my trotting guide, pointing at the sweat that poured from under his helmet. He gave them a surly curse, jabbed his thumb at me and, scarcely breaking his stride, loped back up the hill. I started out onto the pier.

Promptly one of the guards lost his smile as he dashed out of the shack and barred my way with his rifle.

"You cannot go on the pier," he said in Japanese. "It is restricted."

I sighed and put down my duffel bag. A typical snafu deal. It took me twenty minutes to explain everything to his satisfaction. He finally nodded.

"You cannot leave the pier without an approved pass from Colonel Yamata. We have orders to shoot," he said threateningly.

I got up, hoisted my bag over my shoulder, and started down the pier.

Pier 3 was the largest at North Dock. The guard shack was on a small spit of land that jutted out into the North Channel about a hundred feet, with the pier projecting another hundred and fifty feet, roughly toward Manila. It was constructed of heavy planks, about twelve feet wide, with sawed-off telephone poles for pilings. It was a considerable distance from the other piers, which was why, I suppose, it was selected as a mooring point for the barge on which we were to live.

On the right side, a PT boat was tied up to the pilings, its seventy-foot hull wallowing gently on the tide, its guns covered with canvas. I remembered hearing of the valiant duty it had performed against the Jap invasion fleet and how a near miss from a cruiser had damaged its propellers. Apparently the Japs had been unable to repair it.

The living barge, or "casco," as the Filipinos called them, was at the far end of the pier on the opposite side. It was as ungainly as the PT boat was sleek. Short and broad of beam, it tapered bluntly at both ends, and was almost completely covered with a wooden superstructure, crude and unpainted. I jumped down onto the small deck and went in.

It was almost pitch black inside. A wave of stale, stifling hot air hit me as I waited for my eyes to adjust to the gloom. Gradually I began to make out a litter of canvas cots, blankets, and sea bags. Then, seated on a cot at the far end, motionless dim figures came into focus. Two Filipinos were staring at me silently, one of them holding a small mandolin in his hands.

"*Buenos días,*" I greeted.

The mandolin-player just nodded but the other, who I could now see fairly clearly, smiled with a row of even white teeth. He looked considerably younger than his companion. Somewhere around twenty-years old, I judged.

"Good morning, *señor*," he answered in passable English. "You are Lieutenant Sheridan?"

"Yeah; how did you know?"

"The American divers who just arrived yesterday—they were talking about you. I heard them say you would be here today."

I thought that one over. For newcomers to our tight little island, they sure found out things in a hurry.

"Where are they now?" I asked.

"On a work detail, *señor*. Colonel Yamata is in Manila. There has been no diving for three days."

I eased myself down onto an empty cot as I stared at him. "What do you mean—no diving for three days? Who *has* been diving?"

His eyes clouded and his smile disappeared. There was a trace of uneasiness in his voice—or fear. "There were two Filipino pearl divers from Mindanao, and a Japanese navy diver, *señor*. The Jap and one of the Filipinos were killed. The other ran away."

"Killed! How?"

He held his palms up in a gesture of bewilderment, glancing at his companion who watched us silently.

"We are not certain, *señor*," he answered, turning back to me. "Both men were on the bottom when a strong breeze came up. Suddenly the anchor chain parted, and the diving barge heeled over on a wave and started to drift. We pulled up their empty helmets. Their bodies were never found."

"Good God!" I digested this information for a moment. It looked like we were off to a great beginning.

"And who are you?" I asked after a moment. "Are you divers, also?"

"No, no, *señor*. I am Esteban Garcia." He nodded toward the older man. "This is my uncle, Guido Garcia. We are equipment tenders."

"How come you're not out on a work detail like the American divers?"

"But we are not prisoners, *señor*," he protested. "We are civilians. Please..." he stumbled in his effort to explain, holding a hand over his heart in emphasis, "...we do not work for the Japanese because we wish this—but they will not permit us to take other employment. They say they need us—and we both have families to feed."

I looked around at the dark squalor of the casco. "Do you have to stay here? Can't you go back to your families?"

"Only on Friday nights, *señor*. We must be back on Monday mornings."

For Guido's benefit I spoke in Spanish, telling them I understood their situation and felt sorry for them. Then I suggested that we get to work and try to make the casco fit for human habitation before the divers came back. They brightened as though this novel idea would never have occurred to them, and set to work with an almost embarrassing amount of cooperation, making certain each move had my enthusiastic approval.

Although they had been living on the casco for two months, Esteban now made the illuminating discovery that there were several windows on the black walls. He kicked open the wooden shutters that had been nailed shut and sunlight flooded in. It made the place look worse, which, until then, I would have said was impossible.

A few hours later we had sluiced out the interior, scrubbed everything with the stump of a broom, made up the cots, hung up clothes. With light and fresh air streaming in, mingling with the odor of wet wood, it began to seem less like the Black Hole of Calcutta. Stripped down to my shorts—and arm sling—I finally sat down in sweaty exhaustion to survey the result of our efforts. Not too bad. Esteban and Guido plunked down onto their cots, pleased at my smile but obviously a bit puzzled as to the necessity for all the labor. With a sigh, Guido picked up his mandolin and started to strum it softly, his dark, lined face cocked happily to one side. I pointed to the two-burner kerosene stove against one wall.

"Are we supposed to cook on that thing?" I demanded.

Esteban nodded vigorously. "Sí. Each evening, when we come back from the diving, I go to the mess-hall and get food. Guido, he cooks."

"Yeah?" I said skeptically. "What kind of food?"

"Rice and fish. Guido, he is fine cook."

"I'll bet," I shuddered. I was about to go into the matter further when a pounding of footsteps reverberated from the pier outside.

Esteban grinned. "It is the American divers," he said, glancing out the window. "Returning from work detail."

They entered quietly, moving with the sagging heaviness of utter fatigue. Five of them. Their eyes were deep-sunken, dark and expressionless. Glancing about the casco, they nodded with tired approval, then swung back to me with tired curiosity. I could smell the odor of paint that splotched their work clothes with dark green.

The first to enter came toward me with a heavy smile creasing the muscles about his mouth. He had the lithe, muscular build of a middleweight boxer.

"Excuse the paint," he said, holding out his hand. "I'm Frank Stanek. You're Lieutenant Sheridan, aren't you?"

I nodded as I shook the hard grip of his hand. "Jim Sheridan," I corrected, "prisoner-at-large."

His smile deepened and he turned to stab a finger at the other men in rotation. "Nick Borrelli. Don't let his size fool you. He's a hundred and forty pounds of dynamite."

"Wet dynamite, he means," Borrelli interrupted, giving my hand a quick shake. "I never sweat so much in all my goddamned life as I have the last three, four months." He spoke in clipped, nervous phrases from a thin mouth that was overshadowed by a huge beak of a nose.

Frank went on placidly, introducing the others. "The big pile of muscles over there is our beef trust, 'Swede' Anderson. And he's just a shadow of his former self."

The beef trust towered a full head over me, crunching my fingers as a smile flickered shyly on his red, sunburned face. Coarse yellow hair bristled on his head like a recently harvested wheat field.

"Next," continued Frank, "is Karl Fischer. From Prussia, aren't you, Karl?"

Built with a low center of gravity, Karl turned his bullet-shaped head toward Frank with a disgusted snarl. "Von't you effer get it straight? Berne. Berne, Svitzerland." He looked back at me, shaking his head. "Frank choost like to needle me, under-schtand, yah?"

"Yah," I grinned, looking down into his small, stubborn eyes. "I underschtand."

The last of the divers was Morgan Montgomery. He had already flopped down onto his cot with a satisfied groan, having barely enough energy to acknowledge the introduction with a limp wave of his hand. He had a slender, long face and slender, long fingers. Rather handsome, in an effete manner, with curly, black hair; he looked more like a concert violinist than a deep-sea diver, and there was a remote manner about him that, some-how, suggested he was born to the better things in life.

"Sure appreciate your cleaning out this pigsty," Frank said as he stripped off his T-shirt. "Ever since we got here they've kept us busy painting their goddamned barracks. We were too pooped to do anything but sleep when we got back last night." He looked toward Nick Borrelli, who was lying face down on his cot. Swede Anderson was rubbing his back for him. "How do you feel, Nick?"

Nick spoke without looking up. "Great. Just great."

"Guard gun-butted him," Frank explained to me.

This time Nick lifted his head. "Well, they said to paint the whole building."

"Yeah, jerk—but they didn't mean the windows, too."

I couldn't help smiling. Looked like this would be an interesting group. "I got the impression there were going to be six divers," I said. "Did I hear wrong?"

Morgan Montgomery spoke for the first time. There was more than a little sarcasm in his voice. "You heard real good, Sheridan."

Frank spoke up quickly, as though apologizing for Morgan's manner. "There *were* six of us. When the Japs told us, at Cabanatuan, that they wanted us to dive, we told them to go to hell—that it was against the Geneva Convention. They told us the only convention was Japanese convention, and tried to starve us into changing our minds. It was pretty grim for a few weeks. That's why we're in such lousy shape now. When they got tired of starving us, they lined us up in front of a firing squad and said they were going to shoot the whole damned bunch, one at a time. We thought they were bluffing. They weren't. On the first volley they killed Bill Torrence. We decided to go diving."

I nodded silently. Nothing surprised me anymore. After a moment another thought occurred to me. "But when I first heard about you it was all cut and dried that you were to start diving two months ago."

Frank shrugged. "Somebody screwed up. We were put on a boat for Japan. When we got there, though, they discovered their mistake and kept us aboard until they loaded up again. Took us two months round trip." He dropped onto the bunk next to mine with a tired sigh, leaned his back against a rolled-up blanket, and looked at the ceiling with his hands folded behind his head.

The other divers were silent as they sprawled on their bunks, fully clothed. They appeared to be asleep. Guido still plucked at the strings of his mandolin, eyes half-closed as though lost in the rapture of his own music. Esteban had disappeared, taking with him two small pails, and my fervent request that he bring back anything but rice and fish.

Frank turned from his contemplation of the rafters. "Have you been here on Corregidor ever since the surrender?"

I nodded. "Be it ever so humble, it's my home away from home."

"Had any bright ideas on escape?"

"Not very bright. Seems to resolve itself into three possibilities. Steal a boat. Steal a plane. Or swim." As his intent gray eyes studied me, I gave him my original plan to swim across the channel to Bataan. "But," I concluded, lifting my arm in its sling, "I couldn't make it now unless I grew fins."

"Neither could we," Frank said. He ran his palm over the washboard corrugations of his ribs. "In fact, I think only Morgan, Swede and I could make it even if we were in good shape. How about a plane? Can you fly?"

"Only when I buy a ticket."

He groaned. "That leaves a boat as the only possibility. And a fat chance we'd have of getting one."

From the bunk on the other side of Frank, Karl Fischer rolled over and sat up. He rasped a hand over the black stubble on his face thoughtfully.

"How about dot PT boat?" he asked hopefully. "Maybe I could fix it, yah?"

Frank nodded. "If anybody could fix it, Karl could," he said. "He's a world-beater as a mechanic."

I hated to be a wet blanket, but there was no use building up hope on nothing. I shook my head. "The propellers were wrecked by a shell from a Jap cruiser while they were up in Subic Bay hitting an invasion fleet. It was supposed to go with MacArthur's party to Australia, but they had to give it up."

Karl followed through with ponderous logic. "How did dey get it back from Subic Bay? Dot's fifty, seventy-five miles from here."

"This boat, and another one, hid up a river until darkness came. The other gave them a tow back to Corregidor. Guess it was pretty rough for a while. They lost most of their men."

"Goddamn it," Frank swore futilely. "It would have been perfect. We could have run up the coast to Bangar, scuttled her, and cut across, overland, to Bontoc."

I blinked. "What the hell's at Bontoc?"

Frank smiled tiredly and stretched his arms. "Before this mess all started I got well acquainted with a neat bundle of goods named Carlotta. She was secretary to an Admiral at Cavite Naval Base. Her father owns a big plantation just out of Bontoc, and is violently anti-Japanese. While we were in prison camp we heard that a lot of guys escaped through Bontoc and joined a guerrilla army in the mountains of northern Luzon. I'll just bet my bottom dollar that her old man is helping them—he was that kind of a guy."

I sucked in a deep, dismal breath. It seemed so near, yet so far. Just a small matter of transportation.

As Esteban clattered in with his two pails, Nick Borrelli and Morgan Montgomery sat up, starting to gripe before they had their eyes open.

Nick stopped the grinning Filipino and stared down into the pails. "Good God!" he sputtered in his high, thin voice. "Where do you get this swill—off the stern of a ship?"

"It's pelican bait," Morgan informed him. He wrinkled his nose over the other pail. "What's this mess of maggots? Looks like you've got a working agreement with a dead horse."

Esteban's smile grew broader. "But it is only rice, *señor.*"

"Only!" sneered Morgan, his lips curling in disgust. "I'll settle for maggots."

I would have, too, by the time we finished our rice and fish stew.

The following morning, as we were choking down the same unsavory stew and considering pepping it up with a little of Guido's hide—which we finally rejected as being too tough and leathery—we were startled by a heavy bump which shook the casco. Esteban and Guido promptly got up and started for the door leading to the small stern deck.

"What's up?" I asked.

"They have come to take us to the diving barge," explained Esteban. "We are to hurry."

With more curiosity than haste, we strolled out onto the deck and were greeted by the sight of a small, dilapidated fishing boat nosed up against the casco. Its undersized engine chugged despairingly. A hundred feet farther out, hovering in wait, was a trim, gray launch occupied by Japanese soldiers with rifles conspicuously in hand.

"Ah, Guido. Esteban. You have new lambs for the slaughter, yes?" The bellow came from an incredibly fat *mestizo* who was seated at the tiller of the small boat below us. His brown-stained teeth were exposed in a loose, flabby smile. Long, straggly hair left a greasy smear on an impossibly filthy shirt that was once floral-patterned. His fat knees gripped a vodka bottle like a vise.

"My God," I said, staring. "Who is Little Lord Fauntleroy?"

Esteban wrinkled his nose in distaste. "Lucas Reynaldo, *señor.* We call him 'The Pig.' He is hired, willingly, by the Japanese."

As Guido and Esteban climbed down into the fishing boat, a roar of impatience resounded from the launch. It came from a squat, barrel-shaped guard built like a Judo wrestler. Next to him, another guard leveled a rifle in our direction.

From my elbow, Karl spit out one word. "Kempe!"

This was a new one on me. "What are 'kempe'?"

Nick Borrelli answered nervously. "Jap military police. Haven't you run into them before?" He went on before I could shake my head. "Don't frick around with those babies—they mean what they say. Right, Frank?"

Frank nodded. "They think they're God Almighty. Even their officers have a tough time keeping them in line. We'd better get a move on." He dropped down into the fishing boat.

From the launch came another bellow.

"What'd the jerk say?" Swede asked in his soft voice.

"He said to shut up," I translated grimly.

As we sat in silence, trailed closely by the launch, "The Pig" aimed his boat eastward to skirt the high point on Corregidor's long, arching tail. In fifteen or twenty minutes we rounded the point and cut back into the calm, deep water of Caballo Bay.

Ahead of us was the clumsy, dark hulk of a diving tender. It was a wooden ship with a long, pointed prow and a bulbous, low-hung stern. Fluttering canvas canopied all the decks, shadowing the cabins and superstructure so effectively that it was impossible to determine the ship's original lines. Two radio masts speared above it into the brilliant blue sky. Between them, on the bridge, was a huge spotlight. As we approached, I could see long, scabrous strips of dark brown paint peeling from its hull.

"It ain't the Queen Mary, is it?" muttered Nick.

We bumped against the stem and "The Pig" grunted as he tossed a line to a waiting Jap sailor. In a couple of minutes we had boarded the tender and were joined by the guards from the launch, who indicated we were to stay in the stem. The low-slung guard who had bellowed at us earlier appeared to be in command. He had an enormous head set directly on thick shoulders, so that his chin was level with his chest. He was built with all the beauty of a boulder—and looked just about as soft. With narrow-set, suspicious eyes roving over us, he smiled with sadistic pleasure as he barked sharply in Japanese.

"He says to stand at attention," I told the men.

"In this goddamned sun?" snarled Morgan. "What the hell for?"

Nevertheless, he and the rest of us assumed poses that roughly caricatured the kempe's order. Suddenly, from the bridge above us, a tall, thin figure uncoiled from a deck chair with the sinuous flow of a rattlesnake and came to the rail to give us a mocking inspection.

CHAPTER NINE

"I am Colonel Yamata."

As I translated for the benefit of the divers, his eyes swept our group from end to end, horizontally and vertically. They stopped at me.

"Lieutenant Sheridan, kindly take one step forward."

I did.

"You will translate my remarks completely and precisely to assure us of an harmonious relationship." His voice was smooth and cultured, but each phrase was delivered with a rapier-like thrust.

"I am officer in command of the salvage operation. Sergeant Takahito represents the kempe. He has orders to shoot anyone attempting to escape."

A happy smile wreathed the oafish-faced guard, who had stepped back into the shade of the awning below Colonel Yamata.

"Any overt act toward a guard will meet with prompt—and severe—consequences, as I am certain you already realize." He paused to survey us again, his small, aquiline head swiveling slowly on a long, thin neck. Arched forward over the rail with a cold, toothy smile, the resemblance to a snake about to strike was chilling.

"The silver lies directly below us in a hundred and ten feet of water. I am certain you will have no trouble in relocating it quickly. Your quota per man will be two boxes a day. I am not interested in how many dives it will take you to do this."

As I translated this information to the divers, their eyes mirrored the same surprise that I had felt. Esteban had already told us the previous divers had each averaged between three and four boxes per day.

"Now, Lieutenant, kindly call out each man's name and have him take a step forward."

As each diver slouched forward, the Colonel gave him a hard inspection with his glittering, black eyes as though he were taking, developing, and printing mental pictures for his own private rogue's gallery. They shuffled uneasily before this embarrassingly direct examination. Finally satisfied, the Colonel stood up straight and turned back to me.

"That will be all, Lieutenant. Tell them to get to work. They may spend the rest of the morning in checking their equipment, but must commence diving this afternoon. And one more thing—there is to be no talking among you unless it is translated to the guards or myself, and is necessary in conducting your work."

Abruptly he dismissed us by turning back to his chair, which was under a canopy on the upper deck. Coiling himself back into the seat, he picked up a book from a round wicker table and started to read. He looked as relaxed as a lizard on a rock.

We looked at each other in grim silence, then Karl and Swede drifted toward the air compressor mounted on skids near the starboard rail. Guido and Esteban were squatted on their haunches next to the equipment, watching with eyes that were blank and expressionless.

Sergeant Takahito opened a hatch in the bulkhead behind him and motioned inside. I followed Frank, Nick and Morgan into a small storage room, dark and heavy with the dank odor of mold. It was piled with a litter of helmets, hoses, and suits, and belts with heavy lead weights attached. Silently, we dragged several pieces out onto the deck, where I could do nothing further except watch as they began checking the equipment, square inch by square inch. The faces of the drivers grew darker with each inspection. Even to my untrained eye, the suits looked about as safe as diving in a burlap bag. The rubberized canvas was yellowed with age. Crude patches covered much of the original material. Even the patches had patches.

With Guido and Esteban starting to sweat over the ancient hand pump, I got up to peer over the shoulders of Karl and Swede as they studied the pressure gauges. Karl turned his head to look up at me, his mouth clenched in a tight line.

"How deep did he say iss dot vater?"

"A hundred and ten feet. Why?"

"Iss not goot. Don't tink dere iss enuff pressure."

Frank and Morgan looked at each other significantly.

"So that's the reason for the Morse helmets," Frank said slowly.

"Yeah," muttered Morgan. "The divers who were here before us found out the same thing we just did."

I missed the point. "What are Morse helmets?" I asked.

"Not a full suit," Nick answered. "Just a corselet and a helmet. Don't use as much air."

"What's the matter with that? Sounds like a good idea to me."

"It would be except Morse helmets are good only for thirty-six feet. Below that they are suicide."

It was a great choice. Drown in a Morse helmet, or smother comfortably in a full suit.

Suddenly Nick's voice came loud and clear as he held up a split air hose.

"Great gobs of ape dung!" he sputtered shrilly. "Do these Nip bastards think anyone can work with this goddamned junk?"

Starting to turn toward him, a stunning blow smashed against my arm. I spun around, clutching at my arm beneath its sling and swearing at the numbing pain. Takahito's pock-marked face was only a few inches from mine.

"Translate!" he hissed. "Translate as you have been ordered. I will not warn you again."

Rubbing the agony that poured into my shoulder, I gritted out a translation that was slightly inaccurate. "He said the diving suits will need much repair."

Hearing my interpretation, which I gave both in English and Japanese so the divers would understand, Nick composed his face in an expression of evil innocence. "Give the sonuvabitch a swift kick in the nether regions," he said with a pleasant smile.

Takahito stared at me suspiciously. I translated once more. "Also the air compressor is not in good condition."

Nick's smile grew broader. "Tell him I'd like to take his rifle and shove..."

"For Chrissake, Nick," interrupted Frank, "lay off. You're only putting Sheridan on a spot."

Finally Takahito withdrew to the shade of the awning, from where he eyed us and muttered to himself. He wasn't convinced that I was giving him a verbatim translation, but it was too hot to stand in the glare of the sun and argue about it The divers promptly realized this and for the next couple of hours continued their sadistic little game. They quoted from songs, barracks poetry, anything that came into their heads. Each comment brought the sergeant rushing out from his comfortable, shady seat to demand a translation, which the men left up to me to provide, in spite of Frank's irritation. Takahito's face grew red with frustration; sweat gathered in beads on his chin.

Morgan, in particular, kept the game going even though he knew I was almost as fed up as the burly guard. At last I told Takahito I wanted to speak with Colonel Yamata.

"No," he snarled, wiping his face. "He is not to be disturbed."

"It is very important," I insisted.

"I will be the judge of its importance."

I stood my ground, hoping he wouldn't get playful with the butt of his gun. "No. It requires a decision that can be made only by the Colonel."

For a long moment we glared at each other like a couple of unspurred gamecocks, then his eyes flickered and I knew I had him bluffed. Abruptly he wheeled about, motioning me to follow him up the ladder to the upper deck. The divers paused in their work to watch us curiously.

The Colonel was a picture of relaxed contentment. A tall, frosted glass stood beside a chessboard on the wicker table. On the board was a beautifully carved set of ivory chessmen. I observed the set-up with interest, wondering what problem he was working out. He slowly closed his book over a long, tapered finger to keep from losing his place, regarding us with heavy-lidded irritation.

He ignored me and spoke to Takahito in a steely voice. "Sergeant, I thought I made it clear I was not to be disturbed."

Takahito apologized profusely. "But," he added defensively, "he said it was important and would speak only with you."

The Colonel sighed delicately and turned his attention to me, dropping his book in his lap. I saw, by the cover, that it was on elementary chess. Apparently he was trying to teach himself the game.

I took the cold plunge. "Colonel, diving is no snap under the best of conditions, as I'm certain you are fully aware. With the rotten equipment we have to work with, there is much to be done. Complete cooperation must be attained, or there will be a catastrophe. This, obviously, will not further your mission of salvaging the silver."

He lifted a languid hand. "Please get to the point, Lieutenant."

"My point is simply this—if I have to translate every burp and hiccup to your honorable sergeant, the flame of the Japanese Empire will have died in the ashes of history before we get any silver salvaged from Caballo Bay."

A faint gleam lurked behind his obsidian eyes as he digested my lyrical flight. "I am surprised, Lieutenant. I should think you would want to make haste as slowly as possible. Certainly this is better than a prison camp."

"Not a helluva lot," I said flatly. "Diving requires peak physical condition. The men are already suffering from malnutrition and are going to become quick candidates for the bends. Oriental fare of fish and rice does not set too well on occidental stomachs."

Sergeant Takahito, who was listening morosely from one side, spoke up with a snarl. "The American pigs will eat the slop we choose to give them."

Colonel Yamata regarded the source of this unsolicited advice with eyes that bored through the sergeant and came out on the other side. Then slowly he turned back to me.

"Very well, Lieutenant. The men may speak freely among themselves—but strictly on business."

He made this formal by repeating it to Sergeant Takahito, who nodded with a surly grunt, saluted, and went back down the ladder. Turning to me, the Colonel caught my eyes studying the chess pieces. A spark of interest ignited his face.

"You play chess, Lieutenant?"

"Yes," I answered unthinkingly. "And that's a weak opening gambit you're using. Look," I reached out and switched a couple of pieces, "never move your pawns unless you have to—get major pieces out fast for control of the center."

Still talking, I found myself automatically pulling up the other chair on the opposite side of the wicker table and sitting down so I could demonstrate a few points in chess strategy. The Colonel moved up closer and watched with quick interest, asking clarification of a few maneuvers outlined in his book. I soon found he possessed an amazing intellectual capacity for the game, lacking only experience. In an hour of shared common interest, the war came to a temporary halt as far as we were concerned.

Finally I stood up, suddenly aware that I had transgressed the propriety of our military relationship. The Colonel, however, appeared not to give it a thought Or else didn't give a damn.

"Thank you, Lieutenant. Perhaps tomorrow morning you would care to join me for a complete game?"

It seemed like a good idea to find out what made this guy tick. "Delighted, Colonel," I answered.

As I started for the ladder, he stopped me with an afterthought. "I will speak to the commissary this evening," he said, his mouth quirking at the corner. "Perhaps we can arrange for food more suited to Western stomachs. I would dislike to win a game on a physical default by my opponent."

I grinned to myself going down the ladder. I had won one game already.

Reaching the main deck I found Swede Anderson and Nick Borrelli dressed in waist-length corselets from which were suspended lead weights. Frank was screwing Swede's heavy copper helmet into place. They looked at me questioningly.

"You can talk all you want," I said. "I have spake to him and he has seen the light."

"Well," said Morgan with heavy sarcasm as he and Nick joined us, "let's burn incense for small favors."

Nick spoke up in a voice that crackled like small arms fire. "From the length of time you were gone, we thought you were negotiating for the surrender of the Jap navy."

Helmet in place, Swede got up clumsily and went to the stem rail, with Nick following closely. Karl and Frank helped them over the side. In a few moments their figures, blurred by the rippling water, disappeared from sight, leaving only the telltale column of bubbles bursting on the surface. The air compressor "ka-chunked" steadily and rivers of perspiration poured from the backs of the slaving Filipinos.

I learned from Frank that no decompression tables were available. They had had to work one out from memory. At the depth of a hundred and ten feet the divers would spend slightly less time on the bottom than they would in decompressing on their way up to the surface. If they came up too fast they could be crippled or killed by the bends.

Karl stood by the compressor, studying the gauges with a continual shake of his head.

"No goot," he muttered over and over. "Iss no goot."

"What's the matter?" I asked him.

"Dot presshure reading." He stabbed a blunt finger at the gauge. "Iss not satisfactory, yah?"

I resisted the impulse to add "underschtand."

About fifteen minutes later, Frank, who was holding the rope lifeline tied to the submerged divers' waists, shouted over his shoulder at Karl. "They're signaling for more air, Karl."

"No can do," Karl answered grimly. "Better tell dem to come up."

With a curse, Frank tugged on the lines that disappeared into the blue water at a slight angle. "Fine damned mess of equipment," he said. "Rotten suits, rotten hoses—now a pump that won't deliver enough air."

"I never saw a hand-operated pump," I commented. "Thought they were all powered these days."

"They are," he answered shortly. "That hunk of junk over there is an old Navy Mark III. I think it was invented by Leonardo da Vinci."

Suddenly his face mirrored momentary panic. He jerked again at one of the lines.

"What's the matter, Frank?" I demanded.

"Swede has signaled that he's coming up," he answered without looking around, "but I can't get any answer from Nick at all!"

CHAPTER TEN

Tensely, we waited as the minutes crawled by with agonizing slowness. There was nothing we could do but watch the air bubbles rising, expanding, bursting on the surface, as Swede came up in slow stages. He was now at the twenty-foot level where he had to remain for a ten-minute decompression period.

At my elbow, I could hear Karl muttering softly to himself in his native language. I couldn't make out the words. On the other side of Karl, Morgan simply stood, watching the bubbles as though hypnotized.

I turned to Frank. "If Nick won't answer, why don't you pull him up?"

He shook his head tautly. "Worst thing we could do. We don't know what's wrong. He could be pinned to the bottom by falling rock. His lines could be fouled up. If we snapped his air hose he'd be a dead duck."

Tension mounted as we waited for Swede. I glanced behind and saw that the starboard rail was crowded. Takahito was standing next to the compressor, his heavy boots straddling the coil of air lines as he stared intently over the rail. He had been in that position for nearly half an hour. Next to him were three kempe guards, and beyond them were several Japanese crewmen I hadn't seen before—the ship's cook and his helper were obviously by their dirty white caps and aprons, the others were regular sailors. You would think they were watching a grade B movie.

"O.K.," Frank said, signaling on Swede's line by giving it a few jerks. "Time for him to come up to ten feet."

Cold fingers gripped harder at my stomach.

"How much longer?" I asked.

"Fifteen minutes." Frank's voice was curt.

I knew the men could only spend fifteen or twenty minutes on the bottom because of the depth. Nick's time was running out. "Can't you bring Swede up any faster?"

He shook his head without looking at me. "Can't jeopardize one man's safety for another's troubles. Diving is a lonely business."

I glanced at the other divers, beginning to realize what they already knew—if it were possible to help Nick, Swede would already have done so. I leaned against the rail limply.

Karl, who had gone over to the compressor to look at the pressure gauges, came back and tapped me on the shoulder.

"Ask dot Colonel vhere is the nearest recompression equipment."

I nodded and turned to call out the question. The answer was brief. "Manila!"

Frank gave me a hopeless look, his jaw muscles knotted. "It might just as well be in San Francisco," he said heavily.

"Well," I asked, recalling something I had read, "if you have to bring him up too quickly, can't you send him part-way down again to let him decompress normally?"

"Yeah. If he's still alive—and doesn't have water in his lungs. Even then it's not always effective, especially at these depths."

I found my fingernails digging into the wooden deck rail as Swede finally broke through the surface a few feet away from the ship. Karl clambered down onto the ladder, grabbed him by the arm and almost lifted him bodily up onto the deck. I could see his face through the thick glass. It was white with shock. There was complete silence as Frank unscrewed the heavy copper helmet and removed it from the diver's head.

Swede looked up at us unseeingly, then leaned forward with closed eyes and rubbed his hands over his face. He looked up again, swallowed, and tried to speak. His voice came out in a hoarse croak. With trembling fingers he gestured for a cigarette.

I lit one and handed it to him. He grabbed it and inhaled deeply, his shoulders slumped over as he sat on the stool. Then he started to speak, his voice so low we had to lean over to make out the words.

"I don't know what happened. I really don't. I hit the bottom first—landed on a small area of sand dunes about twenty feet east of a steep ridge…

"I looked up and saw Nick coming down on the opposite side of the ridge. The current was pulling him to the west. I started walking parallel to the ridge, figuring he would meet me at the south end, but when I got there I couldn't see him—so I started up the other side. It was rough going—the current through that little gorge is swifter than hell. Then I saw bubbles from near the top of the ridge, on the edge of a big boulder. It was Nick's helmet—just dangling there." Abruptly he stopped.

"Where was Nick?" Frank demanded.

"I don't know. I looked everywhere for him—until I realized it was useless to stay down any longer."

I couldn't figure it out. "What about his lifeline?" I asked. "Isn't it supposed to be for just such an emergency?"

"Yeah," muttered Swede, "but he had tied it around himself in a real loose sling. I noticed it when we were going down. I think it hurt his back when it was tight."

Frank continued to question Swede, apparently not completely satisfied.

"It's damn funny," he was saying. "Nick was too good a diver. How could he just plain fall out of his helmet?"

Swede shook his head. One elbow was propped up on his knee, his hand cupping his forehead. The dangling fingers of his other hand held a forgotten cigarette.

"I don't know. I just don't know," he said dismally. "I had my own hands full." He stopped as a new thought occurred to him. "Say—did anything happen to Nick's air supply? I vaguely remember something odd. I knew he was behind the ridge because I saw the bubbles coming up over the top. Then they stopped. When 1 finally spotted his helmet, though, the air was coming through all right."

"My God!" Frank said, stunned. "If his air supply stopped, his helmet would have filled with water!" He whirled around toward Esteban and Guido, his face black with anger.

Karl promptly stepped forward, holding up a placating hand. "Dey vere pumping all the time, Frank," he said earnestly. "I know because I vass at the compressor all the time Svede and Nick vass below. I had to tighten some loose mounting bolts on the port side."

As Karl cleared the two Filipinos I noted the expression on Guido's face. He was staring, his brown eyes registering paralyzed fear, at Sergeant Takahito who had returned to his seat under the awning.

Frank shook his head. "It just doesn't make any sense. None at all."

Esteban pulled up Nick's helmet and emptied it, the water splashing over the rail and falling back into the sea. He set the helmet down and began to coil up the air hose in a neat pile. The gentle heel of the ship on an ocean swell suddenly caused the helmet to roll across the deck with a ghastly clatter, coming to rest at our feet. The empty glass porthole stared up at us mutely.

We held a brief and simple service. Further diving was suspended for the day and Colonel Yamata allowed us to return to the casco several hours earlier than usual. There was very little conversation, with each man wrapped in the thought of Nick Borrelli's fate. It made for serious thinking.

Later that evening they tried to shake off their pall of gloom by getting up a poker game, playing for matches. I watched for a while, then went over to sit on the bunk next to Guido. He gave me a curious glance as he plucked listlessly at his mandolin.

"What really happened, Guido?" I spoke in Spanish, keeping my voice low.

He averted his eyes, but the grip on his mandolin was no longer casual. "I do not understand, *señor*."

"Yes you do. While Frank and I were at the stern of the ship, Takahito came over to the compressor, didn't he?"

"*Sí.*" I could barely hear him.

"What did Takahito do at the compressor?"

He plucked at the strings of the mandolin without answering.

"You saw Takahito do something with the air lines while Karl was working on the opposite side of the compressor, didn't you?"

He didn't answer. I could see his throat working as he swallowed.

"Guido," I pressed urgently, "you know this is very important?"

He looked up at me pleadingly. "Please *señor*. I do not wish any trouble. The kempe, they are very bad."

"Is your fear so great that you would see the divers die in agony?"

"No, *señor*. I have already seen too much of such things." He laid his mandolin across his lap and leaned forward earnestly. "You will tell no one what I tell you?" Fear etched deep lines in the brown corduroy of his face.

"I swear it."

He took a deep breath. "The Sergeant, he did just as you said. I did not see him until the compressor grew very hard to pump. I looked up and saw him leaning over the hoses, but his back was toward me and I could not see what he was doing. I was just about to tell *Señor* Karl when the Sergeant walked away. I do not know what he did to the hose."

"But the pumping suddenly got easier?"

"*Sí.*"

I nodded grimly. Suspicion confirmed. Or, perhaps I should say that my suspicion that I had a suspicion was confirmed. At any rate, the pieces didn't fit together quite right. First, the Colonel was supposed to be salvaging silver for the Japanese war effort but he didn't bother to provide his first divers with equipment they could operate—and stay alive. Second, without a doubt he was under pressure to bring up the treasure with all possible haste, yet he had reduced the quota for the American divers. Third, there was now little doubt in my mind that Nick Borrelli's death was not an accident. He was much too experienced—he would have been especially cautious on his first dive.

Then, again, perhaps it was all just coincidence, my imagination too fevered. It was certainly difficult to picture the cultured Japanese officer as death in leather puttees—and Takahito as his merciless executioner.

CHAPTER ELEVEN

"Hit the deck, Lieutenant. It's bacon and egg time."

Groggily I sat up with a deep, heartfelt curse. "How the devil can all those wonderful yesterdays become such a lousy today?" I complained.

Swede blinked. Then he wrinkled his perpetually sunburned nose as he tilted his head back to sniff at the air.

"Just smell that," he invited, with rare loquacious humor. "Coffee. Wonderful coffee. Bacon. Gorgeous bacon. Eggs. Beautiful, goddamned eggs." He looked down at me. "Go ahead—smell," he insisted.

Frank came back from the wash basin, wiping his face with a towel. "Do I detect the fine Italian hand of J. Sheridan behind this?" he asked with a broad smile.

I reached for my shoes and socks. "Behind what?"

"The care and feeding of delinquent divers. Guido came back with a fine bucketful this morning."

"Oh. Where the hell is my other shoe? Yeah. I told Colonel Yamata you guys would get the bends on flied lice."

Frank sat down on the edge of his bunk and handed me the missing shoe. "Well, you've endeared yourself to everyone aboard. We're voting you into the Order of the Belching Cockroach."

It was very touching.

The days stretched into weeks as the diving operation settled into a humdrum routine. The enormous pile of boxes in which the silver had been loaded was relocated where they had fallen into a deep cleft on top of a ridge. A line was lowered, with a sling attached, and the boxes were put into it and hoisted to the surface, one at a time. It was soon evident that considerably more silver could be salvaged than the quota established by the Colonel, but the men were more than happy to spend the rest of their time on the bottom in hiding as many boxes as possible in one of the dark caves. Even the boxes that were sent up in the sling were sabotaged by breaking open the ends and letting the silver dribble out in their long ascent to the surface. The Colonel, however, seemed quite satisfied with the results.

My chess games with the Colonel had become about as routine as our trips back and forth to the diving barge. From the first, he had proven a more formidable opponent than I had anticipated. Either he had played more than he admitted or else he learned a damn sight more from books than I ever could. His game was basically defensive; a cunning, waiting game. He protected his king in massed depth, then at the first sign of weakness he would slash out with ruthless ferocity, often taking pieces on an even swap basis. Though weak on experience, he played every game as though supremely confident in complete victory. It was jarring. It took me a long time to spot his weakness. And then I had to drive in with lightning speed to avoid a trap.

One afternoon after a particularly vicious game in which I had had to fight tooth and claw to win the upper hand, he leaned back in his chair and smiled at me—but with his mouth only. I had the feeling he hated to lose at anything.

"My congratulations, Lieutenant. You are an excellent player."

I acknowledged this with a slight tilt of my head. "And you need very little instruction from me, Colonel. I would only question your sacrifice of pawn for pawn when no apparent purpose was served."

He templed his fingers together and the smile glazed on his face.

"Pawns are expendable—in any game. Perhaps I lose strength along with my opponent. But as he becomes unnerved and angry at the senseless slaughter, I become psychologically stronger."

I shook my head in disagreement. "Conservation of strength is a basic tenet."

"That, Lieutenant, depends on the development of the game, does it not?"

An eerie feeling crawled over me with prickly feet. I seemed to be in over my head, without a diving helmet. Cautiously, I tacked the conversation in a different direction.

"Your defense was admirable. Very professional. And vaguely familiar."

He opened his hands with a careless gesture. "I first saw it used in the London tournament while I was attending Oxford. Cardoza employed it to defeat Atherton in 1938."

Suddenly he stopped, a faint gleam of respect in his eyes. "No wonder you are such an excellent player, Lieutenant! That was very subtle."

I lifted my shoulders. "I suspected you could speak English from the beginning, Colonel. It didn't seem likely that American divers would be assigned to an officer who couldn't understand them without an interpreter. And I'm willing to bet every last yen in my pocket you speak better English than I do Japanese."

"You are very diplomatic, also," he murmured. "Hereafter, we shall speak in English. You *do* have quite an accent."

I constantly pushed my unique relationship with the Colonel at every opportunity, needling him for additional concessions. Sometimes successfully—more often not. He did come to realize the necessity for periodic visits to the hospital for treatment of routine diving ailments—arms or legs gashed on the sharp rock, vague aches and pains suffered by the older divers, frequent violent headaches. In fact, we were soon permitted to make these trips without the accompaniment of an armed guard. We had become privileged characters.

On one occasion I made the trip to replenish our exhausted aspirin supply. The doctor on night duty at the infirmary turned out to be the same one who had reassembled me after the last inning of my baseball game. Recognizing me immediately, he seized my left arm and worked it back and forth with a delighted grin.

"Your arm. Not in sling anymore?"

I shook my head. "No. I took it off a couple of weeks ago."

"Good. Good." With a quick fluttering motion, he picked up a tiny examination light and poked it into my ears. "You hear O.K. now?"

"Never heard better." It was useless to tell him I always could.

"That is very good." He stepped back and looked at me with the pride of one who had put together a tough jigsaw puzzle. "Japanese medicine is very good. Yes?"

"Yes." If it weren't for their bad medicine I wouldn't need their good medicine.

I was almost embarrassed to tell him all I wanted was a bottle of aspirin for a sick friend, but I finally managed to state my simple request. He handed me a bottle of something "much better than American aspirin" and I made my escape.

The street lights popped on as I started down the hill and twilight became dark night as suddenly as pulling down a shade. I threaded my way through the streets, surprised to see how the Japs had cleaned and spruced up the area. Buildings had been repaired, bomb craters filled in, debris carried away. I wondered what had happened to all the American prisoners who had done the manual labor at the point of guns.

I had taken a different route back toward the North Dock, where the casco was moored, in order to observe as much as possible, but soon found myself in unfamiliar territory. Many of the landmarks I had once known were gone and were replaced by new ones. I stopped at an intersection flanked by large warehouses to get my bearings.

To my left I heard curt commands barked out in Japanese, and then in the darkness I could make out a small column of men coming up the street from behind a warehouse. I waited.

As they stumbled along under the feeble yellow light suspended over the intersection, I felt a wave of nausea writhing my insides. They were American prisoners, emaciated wrecks, tottering along on spindly legs, swinging stick-like arms. Their once neat uniforms had become travesties—shredded, filthy, flapping loosely on their gaunt frames. A few turned listless eyes toward me as they passed by, and I could see their skulls tautly stretching the sunburned skin of their faces. Death leaned heavily on their sagging shoulders—but they seemed beyond caring.

The column had almost dragged by when one of the stragglers, stumbling and weaving, turned to curse at a guard who was shoving at him with the butt of a rifle. Horrified, I recognized the ghastly caricature of a soldier who wouldn't give up his gun on Bataan. It was Joe Price.

CHAPTER TWELVE

My nerves quivered like telegraph lines in a high wind and my teeth sent frantic gibberish over them in Morse code. But I tried to maintain the appearance of being calm and cool. Swede grinned as he lowered the copper helmet over my head and screwed it into position. Then he opened the faceplate and peered in.

"Everything O.K.?" he asked.

"Yeah," I muttered, "as long as I don't go near the water."

He laughed. "Well, today is graduation day. This is your final exam."

"What if I don't pass?"

"Then you go to the foot of the class."

"Well, as they say, there's always room at the bottom."

Karl, however, took my first dive more seriously. He was as full of advice as a mother seeing her first-born off to kindergarten. Shouldering Swede aside, he gave me last minute instructions. His sober tone made them sound more like last rites.

"Remember. Keep your lines under your arm. That vill keep your helmet from being pulled off your head."

I nodded. "Lines under my arm."

"Never lean over—no more than forty-five degrees, or your helmet vill fill vith vater."

"Right. Forty-five degrees."

"If you pick anything off the bottom—don't bend, squat. Underschtand?"

"Yah. Squat."

I stood up clumsily, feeling the heavy lead weights pulling at my waist, and followed Frank over the rail. I tried to feel cheerful. After all, I was only going a hundred feet. But the fact that it was straight down dampened my enthusiasm.

The water at the surface was as warm as tea and I could feel it boiling over my head as oxygen bubbled from beneath my corselet. Beads of sweat collected on my forehead and ran down my face. Foot by foot, I submerged along the descending line, my hands clamping on the rope like two pair of pliers.

All the water in Caballo Bay was looking for me, crawling up my chest as I descended further, up to my shoulders, then my neck. In a moment of panic, I froze to the line and tried to look upward. Nothing but the pale green of water. I gritted my teeth and forced myself to relax. There was no reason to suck in air with such short, desperate gasps. There was plenty of it coming in a steady, sweet stream. I could almost see Guido pumping with machine-like monotony.

The pale green of the sea gave way to ever-increasing darkness, but when I landed on the bottom I was surprised that there was still enough light to see for several yards. It was like wearing heavily tinted sunglasses. The water was clear, the ocean floor covered with undulating dunes of white sand. A dark hulk looming up a short distance away, looking very much like a sunken ship, startled me momentarily until I finally realized it was nothing more than a mound of black rock worn smooth by the action of eternal, erosive currents.

Frank had waited at the bottom of the descending line. He gave me a close inspection to make certain I was all right, then beckoned for me to follow him across the ocean floor. With only a slight trace of misgivings, I gave up my grip on the line and shuffled after his slowly moving figure.

The eerily beautiful underwater scene would have been a barren, rocky desert up on shore. Nothing but white sand and black rock. There wasn't enough vegetation to make a chef's salad. A few brilliantly-colored fish flashed by in tight formation, like midget racers in their first lap around the track. One of them, a straggler of the non-competitive type, peeled off in a graceful arc and came down to stare into my faceplate. He was disc-shaped with orange and black stripes as bright as a college freshman's sweater. For a few moments he swam backwards, adjusting his rate of speed to mine, and grinned to show me how simple it was. Then, abruptly, he wheeled and gathered speed as he shot upward toward the sheer, black wall of rock that lay to my left. My eyes followed him until he was out of sight.

Turning my head back, I saw that Frank had disappeared ahead of me in the murky gloom. I pushed along as fast as possible, feeling the momentary return of panic. The floor of white sand narrowed until I found myself clambering through a rocky defile that widened after a few feet. Dark canyons of stone converged on me from all sides, and loose boulders cluttered the passageway. I halted, wondering if Frank had turned up one of the canyons, then proceeded straight ahead. If he had altered his course he certainly would have waited until I had caught up with him.

After a few minutes of threading my way through the loose rock, however, my concern began to mount. There was still no sign of Frank. Just as I was about to reverse my direction, I caught the gleam of a metallic object a short distance ahead and slightly to the left of my course. With a sigh of relief, I started after it.

It was soon evident that the reflection was not from Frank's helmet, but my curiosity impelled me forward. The object took shape, suddenly became recognizable as the flank of a submarine torpedo. And piled high behind it was another cargo that had been jettisoned just prior to the surrender—rifles, ammunition, pistols, machine guns, spare parts for boats, trucks, and weapons. It was enough to put a guy in the revolution business.

At the edge of the pile was a rectangular wooden box of the same size and shape as those which had been filled with silver pesos. Wondering how it had become mixed with the cargo dumped from a different barge, I moved up for a closer inspection. Faintly I could make out the black lettering that was stenciled on the side. It was an unopened box of .45 caliber revolvers.

Remembering just in time the injunction, "Don't bend, squat," I groped in the clutter until I found a flat, metal bar and wedged it into the water-soaked lid. The bar buckled under my weight. Disgusted, I threw it down—aluminum, probably a plane replacement part. Further search yielded nothing more adequate than a small boulder, which I used to beat against the corner of the box until the screws were loosened. I ripped up the lid, reached inside and pulled out one of the revolvers. Heavily smeared with a protective coating of cosmoline, it appeared to be in excellent condition.

Now I had to find Frank, and quickly; perhaps I had already spent too much time on the bottom. I stuck the gun inside my waistband under my clothing and turned back in the direction of the descending line. I had barely re-entered the area of ocean floor that was covered by white sand when I saw Frank. He was looking about uncertainly, obviously searching for me. Spotting my approach, he came to meet me and as he drew closer I could see his jaws were clamped with irritation. But his eyes mirrored relief.

I pulled out the revolver and held it up. His brows raised in surprise and his mouth formed a question. I pointed back toward the rocky defile that led to the pile of dumped equipment. He nodded in understanding and, a broad grin breaking over his face, he raised his clenched hands and shook them over his head like a boxer ready for a fight.

This time as he started off he made certain I was behind him—close. He led me around a ridge, and there between high, rocky walls, was a jumbled pile of boxes that stretched as far as I could see. Many of the boxes were broken open from hitting the walls of the canyon on their way to the bottom. Sea-blackened rivers of silver pesos spilled through the pile, filling the interstices between the boxes. Directly ahead was a steel cable attached to a sling arrangement that lay on the ocean floor. The upper end of the cable disappeared into the darkness over our heads. As Frank moved forward and gave the cable a sharp tug, I saw there was a box of coins in the sling. One end was split open.

Quickly the slack was taken in the cable, the box lurched and started its upward journey to the barge moored above us, and coins cascaded silently over the edge, fluttering to the bottom like autumn leaves.

The ascent back to the surface was monotonous, with approximately half an hour of standing in large loops tied in the heavy rope line, waiting to decompress.

I squinted against the harsh light of the sun as Swede pulled me aboard and removed my helmet. Karl handed me a cigarette and surveyed me critically.

"Veil," he said, with one of his rare, fleeting smiles, "how did it go? Vould you like to be a difer?"

I held up my shaking fingers. "It's for men with nerves of steel," I admitted. "Mine are like boiled spaghetti."

"Ach! Dot's nothing. You should have seen me the first time I came up. I had the shakes so bad I couldn't talk for half an hour."

Frank was hoisted aboard and his helmet removed. He turned to me with a glare.

"And how the devil did you manage to get lost?" he demanded. "You weren't five feet behind me when we started out."

"I got to admiring the scenery," I confessed.

"Scenery!" he snorted. "There isn't enough scenery down there to cover a postage stamp."

"Well—there was this little fish ..." I never got any further. And they never let me forget it.

I was impatient to divulge the news of my lucky find to the rest of the divers, but knew it would be too risky until we reached the privacy of the casco. Since ours was the last dive of the day, we cleaned up our gear and stowed it away, then started for the fishing boat already tied up alongside. The gun under my waistband felt as big as a football. I had kept my back turned to the guards as much as possible and Frank, acutely conscious of my hot cargo, had provided me with as much cover as he could. There was no doubt of the consequences if I were caught.

I hoisted one leg over the port rail, preparing to drop into the fishing boat. Suddenly a sharp voice came from the upper rail.

"Lieutenant Sheridan!"

My heart seemed to leap into my throat, then began to pound furiously. I could feel Frank's alarmed glance. Pretending not to hear, I hoisted the other leg over the side.

Colonel Yamata's voice barked louder. "Lieutenant, will you kindly come up here for a moment?"

I wished the fishing boat was not directly beneath me. I would have fallen overboard and dropped the gun into the water. As things stood, I had no choice. Sergeant Takahito approached to enforce the Colonel's command. I turned with sinking stomach and dropped back onto the deck.

Slowly I mounted the ladder to the upper deck where Colonel Yamata waited, his face completely expressionless. I halted on the top step, one foot on the upper deck, and leaned forward with an elbow resting on my upraised knee. I could feel the butt of the gun burning into my belly.

His unwavering stare was as long as a nightmare and almost as upsetting. Then, abruptly, his thin lips parted in a cold smile.

"I merely wish to congratulate you on your first dive, Lieutenant."

My relief was in three-dimensional technicolor. "Thank you, Colonel," I managed.

"I wagered with myself," he went on, "that you wouldn't go through with it."

I inclined my head, not wishing to prolong the conversation.

His smile faded as he studied me. His eyes flickered to my waist.

"Is there something wrong with your stomach?"

"No."

"A touch of the bends?"

"No. It's nothing." He was awfully damned solicitous.

"Perhaps we should have your stomach massaged. It sometimes relieves minor pains from the bends."

"It's not the bends, Colonel."

He inspected me again, then nodded in satisfaction. "I think you just have a case of nerves, Lieutenant."

CHAPTER THIRTEEN

Spirits ran high that evening in the casco after I produced the revolver and described the location and the extent of the resources to be found in the pile of jettisoned equipment. For the first time in weeks, talk of escape dominated the conversation.

Guido, who got a second-hand account from Esteban of my gun-smuggling episode, went to the dark recess behind his bunk and busied himself pulling up a couple of floorboards. In a moment he came over to my bunk and presented me with a bottle of rum and a shy smile.

"I, too, am a smuggler," he said. "This I have saved for a festive occasion."

I was deeply touched. In a short while spirits ran even higher.

Karl Fischer cleaned the cosmoline from the gun with loving care. He held it up and sighted along the barrel.

"Gott!" he exclaimed. "Now ve can get guns, ammunition, and money—all ve need is a goot boat."

Frank nodded. "Yeah. Sure wish that PT boat could be fixed up. They'd have one helluva time catching us in that thing."

Swede grinned. With the help of a few swigs of rum he made what was, for him, almost a filibuster.

"Karl and I looked it over last night. Except for a missing propeller, and a little work straightening out one of the shafts, there isn't a thing wrong with it. Even the gas tanks are almost full."

"Yah," agreed Karl, "and guess what we found under a canvas in the engine room."

"Tondelayo?" I asked hopefully.

"Ach. Even better. A whole case of loaded ammunition belts for the machine guns."

"That's not better, but it's good enough."

Morgan, who generally remained superciliously silent, ran his fingers through his black hair as he spoke thoughtfully.

"How about trying to bribe 'The Pig' with a few smuggled pesos? All that booze he drinks must cost him plenty."

"What have you got in mind?" Frank asked.

Morgan squinted, apparently from the effects of the rum. "Well, he goes into Manila every night. He could buy a propeller, tow it out under his boat when he comes to get us in the morning. Then all he'd have to do is cut it loose when he gets here."

Karl looked up and nodded enthusiastically. "Say! Dot's goot! The guards in the launch vould neffer know vot's going on. We could bring it up at night. The vater here iss only about eight feet deep."

"Risky as hell, though," Frank commented. "I'm afraid 'The Pig' would have a loud squeal."

"You got a better idea?" Morgan asked sullenly.

"I'm afraid not, but …"

Frank never finished his statement. From outside we suddenly heard marching footsteps thundering on the wooden planks of the dock. Karl sat, paralyzed, the gun forgotten in his hand. With a catlike bound, Frank leaped across the aisle, grabbed the gun and thrust it under his pillow. He had barely finished when two soldiers burst through the door, half supporting, half shoving an emaciated figure. With a rough push that nearly knocked their prisoner to the floor, and a few gratuitous insults, they turned and stalked out laughing.

I got up and went over to him. "Hi, Joe. Welcome aboard."

Slowly he sank down on the nearest bunk, the astonished divers staring at him silently.

"My God! Lieutenant Sheridan!" His deep-sunken eyes examined the casco in wonder. "What's this all about, anyway?"

"Didn't they tell you?" I grinned. "You're our new cook."

"Cook!" he echoed incredulously. "Is there something left in the world to cook?"

"Guido," I called out, showing off a bit. "Have we got some chicken left?"

"Chicken!" Joe repeated in awe. "Chicken." His hands shook as he wiped his mouth. "That's a bird, ain't it?"

Quickly I introduced him to the other men, who responded with frank bewilderment.

"Not that we mind a new cook," Frank said, "but—how come?"

"I'm almost as surprised as you," I admitted. "About a week ago I told Colonel Yamata that Joe Price, a veritable Oscar of the Waldorf, was here on the island—and that we would greatly appreciate his services. I also told him it was too much for Guido to pump a compressor all day, then come back and cook for a bunch of hungry men every night."

Frank shook his head admiringly. "You got the guts of a brass monkey."

"Yeah. That's what the Colonel told me. And, among other things, he also said no. I can't figure out why he changed his mind." I turned back to Joe, who was already polishing off a chicken leg. "Do you know who gave the order to bring you here?"

He shook his head as he grabbed for a boiled potato. "Some tall, thin guy with a face like a hungry hawk. He came up to our work party in a jeep about a half hour ago and talked to the guard. They marched me off pronto."

It was Colonel Yamata, all right.

"Where is your duffel bag?" asked Swede.

Joe snorted. "What would I do with a duffel bag—I'm wearing everything I own. The Japs took all the stuff that amounted to a damn. The rest I traded for food. I was beginning to wish I had fillings in my teeth."

"How many prisoners are left on the island?" I asked.

He shrugged. "Don't know for sure. Not many though. Most of them have been shipped out to Cabanatuan or Japan. They kept some of us to work on the roads and the airstrip." He swallowed another chunk of potato before continuing. "It was rough as a cob. They would rout us out at five in the morning and keep us working until dark—sometimes later if they weren't satisfied. And that's been nearly every day lately. We weren't strong enough to do a decent day's work."

I had intended to make another dive the following morning, this time with Morgan, but Colonel Yamata was disposed to play chess. So we played chess. As we set up the pieces on the board, I thanked him for authorizing the transfer of Joe Price to the casco. He acknowledged this diffidently.

A sudden thought occurred to me. Now that Joe Price was assigned to the diving operation, and had no duties other than chief cook and bottlewasher, he would have a lot of free time during the day. It would be nice to have him spend that time acquiring an education—like, what boats were available, how heavily were they guarded, could the guards be bribed. Joe would need a lot of maneuverability. Might as well get the Japs accustomed to seeing him in as many places as possible.

"Colonel, you don't stay on this boat at night, do you?"

"Of course not. I have a cottage in the officers' residential area on the island."

"I see. Very comfortable." I countered his knight's attack on my pawn. "But I suppose you dine at the officers' mess hall?"

"I take most of my meals at the cottage; my maid is also a fair cook—but," he glanced up briefly, "what is the point of this catechism, Lieutenant?"

"I am so pleased at your generous provision of a cook that I thought perhaps we could share his talent with you," I suggested as innocently as possible.

He looked at me blandly. "I'm afraid occidental fare would not set too well on an oriental stomach."

"*Touché.*"

We made several more moves in complete silence. Our games had become pitched battles, fairly well matched. Finally he trapped my queen and leaned back in his chair to enjoy my squirming. He was always full of clever chatter when he had me at a disadvantage.

Smiling faintly, he picked up the frayed ends of our earlier conversation. "I do confess, however, to an inordinate partiality to some of your Western pastries. A corruption I developed while at Oxford. Take a properly baked cherry pie, for example—it can be ambrosia to propitiate the angriest of gods." He sighed. "But your man, judging by his appearance, will be taxed by the effort of warming up a can of beans."

I sacrificed my queen with a brave smile. "We shall see, Colonel..." A sudden commotion from the stern of the ship interrupted me. A hoarse shout of pain counterpointed the sound of feet pounding across the deck.

The Colonel rose from his chair in irritation. "*Now* what is the trouble?" he demanded.

I didn't answer. I was already halfway to the rail.

Below us, two guards had herded the divers against the port rail with their rifles leveled and ready for action. All except Morgan. Apparently he had just come up from his dive. His helmet had been removed but the corselet, with its heavy lead weights, was still over his shoulders, hampering his movements. Spilled across the deck at his feet were several water-blackened pesos. Two more guards pinned his arms against the starboard rail and Sergeant Takahito was beating him with slow, methodical brutality.

Squared off in front of Morgan's writhing body, Takahito leaned his beefy shoulders behind a short, vicious punch deep into the diver's stomach. As Morgan bent over in breathless agony, a slashing judo chop crushed into his shoulder muscle, first on the right, then on the left. Takahito stepped back with a pleased smile and waited for Morgan to straighten up. When he did, his eyes were fluttering; deep, gagging sounds choked up from his stomach. Takahito stepped forward and started over.

"For Chrissake," I snarled at Colonel Yamata, "call him off before he kills Morgan."

The Colonel's answer was as cold and sharp as a razor. "If we weren't so short of divers I would give Takahito my blessing."

After another moment of the inhuman punishment, however, he stopped the sweating sergeant with a curt order. The guards released his arms and Morgan slumped to the deck, sprawling unconscious over the scattered pesos. The other two guards withdrew and the grim-lipped divers rushed over to help the groaning man.

Colonel Yamata spoke with a voice that cracked like a whip.

"Leave him lie!"

Arrested in their tracks, they glared up, their eyes frozen in murderous hate. The Colonel gripped the rail and continued in a lower, almost conversational tone, but his message came through with chilling clarity.

"This is a lesson I want deeply impressed upon you. The next time one of you tries to smuggle silver from this diving operation, he will not only receive similar punishment but will be weighted with a box of silver and sent to the bottom—without a helmet. This, I should like to point out, is a large risk to take by men who are going nowhere, and who can't have any possible use for the silver." He released his grip on the rail and stood up straight. His tone became lighter, almost placating.

"I have done everything to make our relationship a pleasant one; cooperation is very little to ask as your share of the bargain. If you find your duties too onerous, I will promptly grant any request to be returned to Cabanatuan." He stopped and, with a faint quirk on his lips, inspected the divers one by one. There was only stony silence.

"I believe I have made my point clear," he concluded. "Please see that Morgan Montgomery also understands." He turned, gave a pleasant nod, and then disappeared into his cabin.

For several days after his beating, Morgan refused to talk to anyone except Joe Price. Sunk deep in sullen anger, he confided to Joe that the rest of the men had let him down in refusing to come to his assistance. Joe pointed out, uselessly, that it would have meant certain death for everyone. In another week, however, Morgan appeared to forgive, if not forget, but his remarks were limited strictly to swift and terrible vengeance against Takahito.

Joe Price, on the other hand, improved rapidly. For a time, he spent most of his waking hours shoveling food into his face with the single-mindedness of a stoker-fed furnace, but as his thin frame began to fill out he proceeded, with the same interest, to develop another talent—scrounging.

With the aid of the pesos we managed to smuggle in spite of Colonel Yamata's warning, all sorts of creature comforts made their appearance in the casco; a large green carpet that had once adorned General MacArthur's cottage, a choice library of books that the Japs couldn't read, a small bar that was, mysteriously, very well stocked, a few potted plants, medical supplies, the choicest cuts of meat. And he worked for two weeks on his greatest accomplishment—a power line from a nearby generator on the island. Shortly after that we had electric lights and a small refrigerator. Our dingy casco had become a luxurious cruise ship.

The first evening that Joe returned from Colonel Yamata's cottage, having delivered a few cherry tarts, his eyes were glittering with excitement.

"Wow!" he announced enthusiastically, "have I got something to tell you!"

"The war is over?" Frank guessed.

"Aw, cut it out. No. I just found out that the Colonel's maid is, or was, the wife of a Filipino diver who worked on the salvage job before you guys started. He was killed when the anchor chain parted. Man, how she hates Japs!"

"So how come she's vorking for one?" asked Karl, unsympathetically.

"Well, he offered her a job. Felt sorry for her, I guess. She took it thinking she could strike a blow for liberty or something. Her name is Rosita," he added irrelevantly.

"She could try a little arsenic in the Colonel's soup," suggested Morgan.

"Yeah," laughed Joe. "I already thought of that when I was baking the cherry tarts."

Frank held up his glass. "May I have a bit more wine, Mr. Price?"

"But of course, Mr. Stanek." Joe tilted the bottle, filling Frank's glass.

Frank reached out, clutching Joe's arm, and read the label on the bottle.

"Nineteen thirty-four—a Very poor year. May I suggest the 1937 vintage when you go to the store tomorrow?"

"I'll put it on my shopping list," Joe promised. He looked around the table solicitously. "Anyone for caviar? They are having a special—two pounds for seventy pesos."

Swede sighed heavily. "Much too expensive, Mr. Price."

"Yah," agreed Karl. "The cost of liffing iss certainly getting terrible. By the vay, tomorrow iss payday. How much vill you need for expenses?"

Joe put down his fork and patted his mouth delicately. "Well," he said, staring at the ceiling in heavy thought, "there's two hundred pesos for our bootlegger, fifty for utilities, another hundred for the butcher—I think I can get by with about seven hundred pesos if I watch my budget."

Frank nodded in satisfaction. "That's what I like—a good money manager."

Joe shook his head gravely. "Jeez, when I think how good we've got it..." He stopped and swallowed, then went on. "I saw one of my buddies today. He doesn't look like he's going to last another week."

"Where did you see him?" I asked.

"At the Colonel's cottage. He was on the garbage detail."

I looked up. "He was picking up garbage at the Colonel's place?"

Joe looked at me wonderingly. "Yeah, Why?"

A sudden vague thought began to take shape. "How do they pick up the garbage—in G.I. cans?"

The other men stared at me, sensing my excitement.

"Sure," Joe answered. "How else? This girl I was telling you about—say, is she ever a knockout! She..."

"Never mind about her," I interrupted impatiently. "Tell us about her later. How does this garbage detail work?"

"Well, same as any garbage detail, I suppose. I'm no expert. She takes the kitchen garbage out to the big G.I. can in back of the cottage. The prisoners pick it up in a truck and take it away. Period."

"That's it!" I exclaimed. "Our pipeline! Joe bakes two pies for the Colonel. The guards scarcely pay any attention to Joe anymore, so he gets by them easily. He delivers the pies to the Colonel's cottage. His cook dumps one of them into the garbage, and the prisoners pick it up."

"Big deal," announced Morgan. "Garbage pie!"

"Yeah," I answered. "Garbage pie full of pesos—for the prisoners to buy food and medicine!"

To a man they rose and toasted me with wine. Nineteen thirty-four vintage, though.

CHAPTER FOURTEEN

Our silver-smuggling operation grew to an awesome production rivaling the Comstock lode. In fact, we were much more efficient. The pesos were immediately negotiable. As reports filtered back to us through our pipeline from the astonished prisoners, we were inspired to even greater efforts with the knowledge that the blackened pesos had spelled the difference between life and death for many of them.

Strangely enough, Sergeant Takahito never bothered to search us, apparently feeling the beating he had administered to Morgan had effected a permanent cure. Nevertheless, we exercised prudent caution. Swede contrived an ingenious arrangement with an old gas-mask bag tied to a line and suspended from the port side of the diving tender next to "The Pig's" fishing boat. The other end was slung under the ship and tied to the descending line. As the divers came up the line, they would fill the bag with pesos and then swing it loose. When none of the guards was watching, the bag would be pulled to the surface and smuggled into the fishing boat, then removed as we disembarked at the casco. "The Pig" was never a threat. The alcoholic fog surrounding him was two quarts thick and ninety proof wide.

Karl spent all his free time on the PT boat, checking every mechanical detail with loving care. His job was somewhat complicated by the fact that he could only work under cover of darkness to avoid detection by the guards. For the same reason the rest of the men avoided the boat as much as possible, except one of us would go with him when he needed help. On one of these occasions I held a flashlight while he cleaned and checked the fuel lines.

"How far do you think our gas will take us?" I asked in a low voice. "It'd be tough paddling this baby."

He shrugged. "Hard to say. If ve could run all three engines she vould develop about four thousand horsepower—and hit sixty miles an hour. That takes a lot uff gasoline."

"What do you mean, *if* we could run all three engines?"

He shook his head. "Dot middle shaft iss so badly bent I can't straighten it vith these tools. Ve'll haff to get along on chust two."

"That's just great," I muttered. "I suppose that'll cut our speed down to around forty miles an hour."

He nodded. "Yah. About that. Ve vill haff to depend on the element of surprise and get as much head start as ve can."

I turned and looked up through the hatch at the twin mounted machine guns bulging under their canvas covering.

"We'd better have those guns ready for action. I have a hunch there's going to be fireworks when we punch out of here."

"Yah, I haff already checked them. They are in goot condition." He slid a brass nut down over the ferrule and screwed it back into position. Then he squatted back on his haunches with a satisfied grunt and glanced about in the dark shadows of the hold. "Vell, that takes care of about everything; fuel lines, electrical system, steering gear …"

"How about the radio?" I asked.

"Ach! Vot do you vant to do vith a radio? Listen to Tokyo Rose?"

"No. I'd just like to find out if the United States is still fighting this war—and if so, where. I get a lonesome feeling now and then."

He laughed shortly. "Pretty soon ve vill get lots uff attention. You von't be lonesome. All I need now is a propeller and then ve are on our vay. Haff you talked to 'The Pig' yet about getting us one?"

I shook my head. "We've got a better arrangement. Guido and Esteban have volunteered to buy one in Manila."

"Dot's goot. But how are they going to bring it to the casco?"

"Well, they know where 'The Pig' moors his boat on weekends. They're going to tie the propeller under it while he's off on a saloon circuit and let him bring it out the next day without him knowing anything about it. When he gets to the casco we'll cut it loose just like we originally planned."

"Dot's much better. That drunken souse vould betray us to the Japs for a bottle of gin."

But it wasn't as simple as it sounded. Propellers for U.S. Navy torpedo boats weren't carried in dime stores. Guido and Esteban spent several week ends searching with dogged persistence through all the marine supply stores in Manila, but invariably returned to the casco to report their fruitless efforts with prolonged and painful detail. Our spirits began to sink like punctured tires.

It was late Saturday morning. Frank and I had assumed our usual positions, perched on the stern rail of the casco, and were watching the seagulls as they wheeled through the blue sky. Below them the surface of Manila Bay lay as smooth as a cauldron of molten gold. A soft breeze fanned across our faces from the south, giving me the second-hand luxury of Frank's bulldog pipe.

"What do you burn in that thing?" I demanded. "Fish glue?"

He ignored the slight. "It'll soon be typhoon season," he commented placidly.

"Great. I'm getting tired of this beastly weather."

"Yeah. But it could foul up our escape plans. Handling a PT boat in a typhoon could be a rough proposition."

This was a sobering thought. A seventy-foot boat would ride like a bar of soap in a washing machine. I was about to answer when a clattering of feet on the dock interrupted our conversation. Frank twisted around for a better view.

"It's Esteban and Guido," he announced in surprise. "I never saw Filipinos move so fast."

I joined him at the port rail to watch them shuffling toward us at a half-dogtrot, their faces ruddy with exertion.

"And on Saturday morning," I said, equally surprised. "They never come back before Sunday night."

In another moment they clambered over the rail, their faces alert with the eager anticipation of two hound dogs who had just treed a nice, fat coon.

"Ah, *señor*," panted Esteban, "it is great good news that we bring."

"*Sí, sí*" Guido interposed happily. "The stars have shone on us today."

Esteban interrupted impatiently. "It was only this morning that I said to Guido ... let us go to the church and pray to the Holy Mother and light many candles ..."

"And maybe she will listen and answer our prayers," finished Guido triumphantly.

I shoved them inside the casco where their voluble chatter wouldn't attract the attention of the guards at the other end of the dock. Joe, Swede and Karl looked up from their game of rap poker as we entered. Morgan, who was lying on his bunk and staring at the ceiling, hoisted himself up on one elbow. The sight of the two normally unobtrusive Filipinos literally dancing with excitement provoked as much interest as a bevy of chorus girls from a burlesque show.

"Now," I said, firmly pushing them down on a bunk, "will you please speak slowly? You are already two laps ahead of me."

Esteban took a deep breath and managed to break away from the post a little faster than Guido. To the irritation of the other men, however, he spoke in Spanish to make faster headway.

"And then, *señor*, just as we were leaving the church, who should we meet but the cousin of my sister-in-law's uncle."

"No!" I breathed reverently.

"*Sí*, it is true. And who should he be working for these past two months—Pancho Morales!"

"But he does not work too often," interjected Guido quickly. "Because he has gone to school, this cousin of Esteban's sister-in-law's uncle, and he is very smart. He spends much of his time just thinking."

"*Sí*," nodded Esteban in sober agreement. "In the Villa Rosa beer garden."

"For God's sake!" groaned Frank. "Will you please tell us what these two characters are jabbering about?"

I brought them up to date in short order. "Esteban and Guido met a guy on the church steps this morning."

Esteban blinked, both startled and pained at such rapid translation of their vital information, then continued: "Now this Pancho Morales, he is the owner of a very large scrapyard next to the Pasig River. He buys many things..."

"Many, *many* things," Guido corrected, with a frown.

"*Sí*, that is so—many, *many* things. And when we tell the cousin of my sister-in-law's uncle about the thing for which we are searching, he takes us to the great scrapyard of Pancho Morales."

Guido dove in as Esteban paused for breath. "And there we meet Pancho Morales himself!" He turned to Esteban for confirmation that this amazing event had actually occurred.

Esteban confirmed, nodding his head with such animation that the bunk shook beneath them.

I turned to the men, who were fidgeting around us, barely able to contain their impatience.

"This guy they met took them to another guy who owns a scrapyard."

Esteban clearly indicated that the full flavor was being lost in my translation, but he bravely continued: "Then we tell Pancho Morales of the thing for which we seek and he tells us right away that he has such a thing..."

"What!" I interrupted excitedly.

But Guido quickly shook his head with a mournful expression. "But we have heard that one cannot always believe Pancho Morales. Whatever you want, Pancho Morales will say he has it—even though he does not."

"Oh."

Esteban brightened, however. "So we, ourselves, Guido and I, we go out into the scrapyard among the many, many things…"

"Yeah, yeah." I could have clubbed both of them cheerfully.

"And we find that Pancho Morales has purchased a whole barge load of scrap from the Japanese which came from Cavite Naval Base. And there among the many things is that which makes the boat go—a great shining propeller of the proper size!"

I could feel a big smile splitting my face and I looked at the rest of the men.

"Hang onto your hats," I said. "Guido and Esteban have found a propeller that will fit the PT boat!"

It took fifteen minutes to calm them down. I didn't blame them. I felt the same way. Our escape plans had taken a great jump forward from vague dream to solid possibility.

"How much does this guy want for the propeller?" Frank asked.

"Two hundred pesos, *señor*," answered Esteban. "That is why we have come back today… to get the money and return to buy the propeller quickly."

Frank pondered for a moment, then shook his head. "Too risky. The guards will wonder why you are going to Manila twice in one day. Better wait until tomorrow morning. They will expect you to go to church."

"And argue with Pancho Morales about the price," I suggested. "He'll wonder where you got all the money if you don't."

Guido looked dubious. "But we have already given him fifty pesos to hold it for us."

"Did he ask why you wanted the propeller?"

"*Sí*. But we told him a friend of ours had purchased a fishing boat and would give us jobs if we could find this very rare item."

"Excellent," I commended. "How about 'The Pig's' boat? Do you know where it is?"

Esteban nodded. "And he is already very drunk, *señor*. He has been drinking since early last night. Tomorrow night we will tie the propeller under his boat and then we will come out with him Monday morning to make certain everything is all right."

It sounded foolproof. In high spirits we turned to the question of figuring out how Guido and Esteban would carry the balance of one hundred and fifty pesos that was needed to make the final payment on the propeller. Since the coins were large and heavy, carrying so many at once was a perplexing problem. The fifty pesos they had already given Pancho Morales had been smuggled into town over a period of several weeks, a few pieces at a time.

Finally it was decided. On Sunday morning we took a mattress cover and tore it into four-inch wide strips. The strips were folded and wrapped around both Guido and Esteban from waist to chest until they looked like sweating mummies, then we inserted the pesos into the continuous slot formed by the folds. After they replaced their clothes, the bulkiness of the swathing was undetectable. Except for a slight stiffness which showed only when they sat down, it was an ideal arrangement.

At last all was ready. Each of us bade Esteban and Guido a fervent "*vaya con dios*" and watched as they awkwardly climbed up onto the dock and stalked toward the guard shack. The guards waved them by. We began to breathe again.

The rest of the day passed with the speed of a hundred-car freight train on an August afternoon. Our usual Sunday chores around the casco were performed in preoccupied silence, and the remaining hours were spent aimlessly, restlessly. Night came. Uneasy premonitions hung in the darkness like the shifting shrouds of the aurora borealis. After our usual late-evening cup of coffee, we silently hit our respective sacks.

The sound of marching feet tramped with crude unfeeling through my soft, warm dream. Until I finally realized they echoed from the dock beside the casco. Quickly I shoved my feet into my shoes and shook Frank's bunk at the same time.

"Hey, wake up. Here come Esteban and Guido."

He promptly sat up, displaying his remarkable ability to hurdle from deep sleep to complete, oriented attention.

"How come?" he asked, frowning at the footsteps. "Thought they were coming in the fishing boat."

"Yeah," I said. I froze in the act of tying my shoe. "You're right, they were."

Something was wrong, very wrong.

I pulled on my pants and headed for the door. The other men were groggily coming to life, groaning and cursing at the start of another day.

I stepped out onto the stern of the casco and turned toward the dock. Directly in my line of vision was a pair of highly-polished leather boots encasing whipcord breeches. My gaze traveled up the knife-edge press, up the open-throated khaki shirt, into the coldest, deadest eyes I have ever seen. It was a captain of the kempe, swagger stick in one hand, a drawn pistol in the other. Behind him were four kempe police. Their rifles were aimed at my stomach.

"Inside!" the officer commanded.

Slowly I backed through the doorway into the casco as he dropped lightly to the stern deck, followed by his guard detail. The men inside, not yet fully dressed, stared at us in open-mouthed, shocked surprise. The captain strode the length of the casco with stiff military precision and seated himself at the table, the rigidity of a West Point lower classman in his bearing. Two of the guards stood at parade rest behind him, their eyes wary, while the other two flanked the open doorway.

The captain stared about the casco, taking in our accommodations with sneering arrogance. Then he spoke, his voice as pleasant as the bark of a hyena.

"Just what I would expect of soft, luxury-loving Americans. Carpet on the floor, pictures on the wall, even..." he stopped, goggle-eyed, "a *refrigerator!*" Words failed him as he choked up, his face changing color. "You call yourselves soldiers? I suppose you keep choice wines in your refrigerator?"

No one answered. It was a time for prudence.

He suddenly slapped his hand on the table with a cracking report that made us jump in unison.

"Esteban Garcia and Guido Garcia!" he shouted. He stopped and stared at each of us in turn, looking for some reaction. But sudden, welling dread had petrified our faces.

"Caught!" he bellowed after a moment. "In the crime of stealing from the Imperial Japanese Government."

"What did they steal?" I managed to ask.

His ugly frown gave way to an uglier smile. "You think you can fool kempe? No one can fool kempe. You know very well they were attempting to smuggle silver pesos into Manila. They have confessed that you helped them." Again he surveyed us, one by one, a gloating grimace on his round face, then he pulled a sheaf of papers from his inner pocket and placed them with neat precision squarely in the center of the table. Next to them he laid a fountain pen.

"Now," he said, springing back to his original position like a piece of tempered steel, "I want a signed confession from each of you, admitting complicity."

"Why the hell should we sign anything?" Frank demanded, having gained some sense of composure although his face was still pale with apprehension.

The captain turned to him and snapped, "Because you have already been warned of the serious consequences. If you are not stupidly obstinate we may prove to be of a lenient turn of mind."

"How about Esteban and Guido?" I asked.

"They will be dealt with in the proper manner. Their fate should be of no consequence to you."

"But it is," I insisted. "Even if they did take a few lousy pesos what difference does it make? There are millions upon millions more where they came from."

He answered me, chopping off each word with a heavy, meat-cleaver voice. "It makes a great deal of difference. So many silver pesos have already been smuggled into Manila that the Japanese occupation currency has been seriously undermined. Our soldiers are finding that their month's pay will scarcely buy a cheap bowl of rice. The merchants in the city prefer the silver to paper money. It is sabotage in its most vile form—and will be stopped at all costs!"

We refrained from looking at each other, but all the divers realized what had been happening. The flood of pesos we had smuggled through to the American prisoners eventually found its way into the hands of Jap soldiers and Filipino workmen who had carried them into Manila in a never-ending stream. We hadn't dreamed that our scheme would backfire so monstrously.

Our attempt to argue with the implacable kempe officer was cut short. The fate of Esteban and Guido had been sealed, and nothing we said or promised could make the slightest difference. Impatiently he rapped on the pile of paper, exasperation tightening his lips.

"Now, I want these papers signed at once. I have no more time to waste in useless conversation."

I shook my head. If they were positive of our complicity they wouldn't bother with the formality of our signatures. It was worth a bluff.

"Captain," I said harshly, "there is no point in attempting to frame us. What useful purpose would it serve? Besides, as you are aware, the vast bulk of the treasure is still on the ocean floor. Who will bring it up? Your own divers are urgently needed elsewhere."

For a long, uneasy moment he stared through me, his face as immobile as a death mask, then he slowly reached for the stack of papers and refolded them. I could feel the tension running out of me like sand through an hour glass. It was an effort to keep my shoulders from slumping.

"Very well." He stood up and surveyed us haughtily. "You are most fortunate that we are fair and just. I am still suspicious even though the two Filipinos support your story, but lacking evidence I will accept the fiction of your innocence—for the time being." He paused for a moment, then added, "To make this an unforgettable lesson, you are all to assemble on the dock at once."

He stalked through the door, the four guards prodding us after him with their guns. With heavy foreboding, we filed out and climbed up onto the dock where the guards shoved us in a line facing the shore.

Joe turned to me, his jaw muscles quivering as he controlled his fear.

"Are they going to shoot us?"

I shook my head without looking at him. "No. But I almost wish they were."

On the rocky shore, just past the guard shack, another group of kempe guards surrounded Esteban and Guido. They were scarcely necessary. The two Filipinos looked as if they couldn't have walked ten feet. Their hands were tied behind their backs and they had been stripped to the waist. I could see flies swarming over the raw, red welts and dark crusted blood that covered their limp shoulders. Someone groaned an involuntary curse as Esteban turned and, seeing us, lifted his head a little higher.

The captain marched up the dock with his four guards and spoke to those in charge of the prisoners. I couldn't make out his words. Sick horror gripped us as we watched the terrible tableaux unfold beneath the merciless tropical sun. The guards moved back a few paces and leveled their rifles. Esteban and Guido were forced to kneel on the rock, facing the placid blue sea. The captain took out his pistol and with slow deliberation checked it carefully and then held it to Guido's head. I closed my eyes. The explosion came, echoing dully against Malinta Hill. Then another.

It was all over. We stumbled back into the casco.

"My God!" Morgan's voice was choked. "Not even the honor of a firing squad."

Swede shook his head blindly. Picking up Guido's mandolin from his empty cot, he strummed a tuneless chord, then carefully hung it over a nail on the wall. We sat on the edge of our bunks and stared at it.

CHAPTER FIFTEEN

The days went by and somehow we stumbled through them. Gloom smothered us like a hot, steamy blanket. Not only did the death of Esteban and Guido weigh heavily on our conscience, but with them died the plans for escape that had come so close to realization.

Colonel Yamata was fully aware of our mood and left us strictly alone, even though production dropped as low as five boxes of silver a day. Since the divers were now forced to man the air pump themselves, we had a ready excuse available for the poor showing.

After a week of this, Colonel Yamata summoned me to the upper deck.

"Lieutenant, the morale of your compatriots leaves much to be desired. While I feel great sympathy for the loss of Esteban and Guido, I also have a job to do—and it is not being done. The Japanese High Command has been asking some very upsetting questions, and has threatened to replace you men with native divers from Mindanao. I am certain you appreciate the gravity of this."

I nodded silently.

He went on. "In return for a promise to improve our record, I am prepared to grant a rather extraordinary privilege. Today is Friday. At seven this evening, assemble at the guard shack on the dock. I will then take you into Manila for a week end of relaxation!"

I was slack-jawed with astonishment.

It took me a full hour that evening to convince the rest of the men that I wasn't pulling their collective legs. Not until I started to get myself dressed up did they really believe me.

"I don't get it," Frank said with a puzzled frown. "First these Japs blow hot, then cold."

I nodded. "Because we are the enemy—undesirable, but indispensable."

"Indispensable? Like Colonel Yamata told you…they can always get native pearl divers."

"Yeah. But I think the friendly Colonel doesn't want any of the native divers on the job. I think there's method in his madness…" I was interrupted by shouts and laughs as the other men piled out through the door and swept us before them. We were on our way to a party. Or something.

We were met by Colonel Yamata and a six-man kempe guard detail led by Sergeant Takahito, and taken by truck to the south docks, where we were hustled aboard a native schooner. It had been converted to a troop ferry, plying Manila Bay between Corregidor and Manila. The speed with which it panted and groaned toward the city scarcely took your breath away.

Frank slipped into the seat next to me and spoke in a low voice. "Sheridan, I think you're onto something. What did you mean by your statement that there was method in Yamata's madness?"

I shrugged my shoulders, not really knowing what I had meant. It was just a hunch. The kind that sometimes makes you certain you're going to roll snake-eyes with the dice when you've got a big bet down on the table.

"I don't know for sure, Frank. But if I can only find out what happened to that native diver who ran away before we came on the diving scene, it might help me prove a point. Costeau knows everybody—I'll get him to work on it right away when I see him."

At the Manila dock we transferred to trucks again and in half an hour rumbled up to the entrance of the Casa Grande. The doorman took a dim view of the Jap guards who came spilling out. He spit on the sidewalk and stalked inside, probably to warn Costeau of the invasion.

As we jumped down, Colonel Yamata called to me from his command car. I went up to him, noting that Sergeant Takahito was acting as his chauffeur.

"Lieutenant," he said, "I hope this does not disappoint you greatly, but Sergeant Takahito and I will be unable to join you. It is unnecessary to point out that I have placed you on your honor to do nothing...impetuous."

I glanced at the string of guards who had already taken up strategic positions. Some had disappeared around the corner to watch the side and rear of the hotel. I gave him a cool smile and said, "You place a high value on my honor, Colonel."

"Their presence should be a relief to you," he answered shortly. "If one man attempts to escape you will all suffer the consequences. This impartiality may not comfort *you*, but it will comfort *me*. Another chess player such as you would be difficult to find." Takahito crashed into gear with sledge-hammer finesse, the Colonel nodded a cynical smile at me, and the command car roared off with a lurch and a squeal of tires.

The rest of the men were impatiently waiting for me in the lobby, scarcely aware of the astonished looks from the hotel guests and management. The Filipino doorman, who had been chattering volubly with the desk clerk, turned toward us and dropped his jaw as he took in our uniforms. He walked slowly toward us as though expecting we would vanish in a cloud of smoke.

"*S-s-s-señors*," he stammered, blinking. He looked behind us. No Jap guards. "*S-s-s-señors*," he tried again. "I don't understand."

Joe stepped up and clutched him by the arm. "Say, Mac," he asked in a hoarse stage whisper, "you don't happen to know where we could get a couple of tanks and a few machine guns, do you?"

"But, but no, *señor*," the doorman answered, completely rattled. "This is just a hotel. We have no, no ..."

"Ain't this General MacArthur's headquarters?" demanded Swede truculently.

The doorman was getting a bit limp. "No, no. This is the Casa Grande." Helplessly he looked around for assistance.

"I *told* you guys." Joe turned an indignant expression on us. "MacArthur went south, just like those fellows said."

"Veil," said Karl ponderously, "ve might chust as veil go into the bar and drink until the Japs decide to surrender."

We were off to a great start.

Frank and I went to the desk, where we attempted to make known the fact that we wanted to register for the week end. The other men trooped with unerring instinct in the direction of the casino. The Chinese clerk simply stared at us with glassy eyes. Just as I reached out to swing the guest book around, a bellow of rage came from the direction of the marble stairway.

"Wong! Wong, where the devil are you? What are those filthy Japanese soldiers doing outside my hotel? *Sacré!* I've told you a hundred times ..."

With the gentleness of an avalanche he roared around a potted palm toward the paralyzed desk clerk. In passing, his glance swept over us, flickered to a stop, then incredulously moved back. A huge smile grew on his face, big as a sunflower. I braced myself.

"But it is impossible!" He pivoted around, lunged in my direction and hoisted me six inches off the floor in a crushing embrace. "It *is* you, my old one." Holding me at arm's length like a rag doll, he surveyed my slightly crushed frame. "And looking so good. Where have you been? What have you been doing? What are you doing here?"

I struggled feebly. "If you'll only put me down so I can practice breathing again I'll tell you."

He set me down gently as a Ming vase and I introduced him to Frank, who covertly checked his fingers after rescuing them from the muscular innkeeper's grasp. Costeau quivered his mustachios with delight as I explained the circumstances leading to our visit.

"But we didn't have time to make reservations," I concluded hopefully.

"Ah, my good friend, Jacques Costeau always has room for his friends when they decide to take a vacation from the war. I will arrange things immediately."

He turned to the desk clerk and I looked around for Frank. I was just in time to see him disappear into the casino, holding the arm of a pretty Filipino girl. A man of action.

A moment later Jacques and I also went into the casino and found a secluded pair of seats at the end of the bar. The bartender lifted his brows when he saw me and automatically reached for a bottle of rum. It was like coming home. I looked around the crowded room appreciatively.

"Well, Jacques," I grinned. "Looks like the war has detoured the Casa Grande."

His mouth tightened as he answered. "We have had a few minor skirmishes, old one—but we have managed to repel the invader, so far. Somehow, the Japanese soldiers find it difficult to get waited on. And when they do, it is quite impossible to remember which one has given us the money. Once in a while an officer comes in, but even their money buys very little. They don't stay long."

"That reminds me," I said, "there is some information about a native diver that I must have very quickly—and it is very important."

"Just tell me what you wish to know, my friend. I will move heaven, earth and a large portion of hell to find out whatever it is."

As I told him of my suspicions, and the reason for my request, his face grew dark.

"But it is fiendish," he said in a voice heavy with loathing. "And completely possible. I will start an investigation for you immediately."

He left his drink and headed for his office. While he was gone I spotted Joe and the divers at a large table in an alcove across the murky room. Even from where I sat it was easy to see they were making very good use of their time. With great regard for equality, justice and fraternity, there was a girl seated between each of them, doing her noble best to ease the lot of the fighting man. I thought it quite admirable.

Jacques returned and picked up his drink. "It is done," he announced with satisfaction. "We shall soon know."

This, too, was admirable. Also it made me curious.

"How do you get this kind of information?" I asked.

"Simple, my friend. I know a detective on the police force. When he is on duty he dines in our restaurant regularly. He owes me a favor."

As I listened, I tilted my glass and suddenly found the cool liquid running down my chin as a heavy thump landed between my shoulder blades. Looking around in irritation, I found Morgan standing at my elbow. He was weaving uncertainly, his eyes feverishly bright. Holding up his own empty glass in a mock toast, he addressed me loudly.

"Well, if it isn't our silver-tongued spokesman, the army's gift to the Godforsaken, liberator of the legion of the lost. Come tilt the cup with old Morgan-of-the-deep Montgomery."

He was canned to the eyebrows. With his lean face set in a sardonic grin and his curly, black hair ruffled into peaks on either side of his forehead, he looked like an alcoholic Mephistopheles.

I managed what I hoped was a pleasant smile. "I'll be over in a few minutes," I promised. "And save a little for tomorrow," I added, glancing at his glass. "We have a full week end ahead of us."

He focused his eyes on me with some difficulty. "Time and tide wait for no man," he proclaimed sonorously. "Besides, the scotch can't possibly last as long as my money will."

I looked at him in alarm. "Good God, what *are* you using for money?"

He held up a finger and waved it, a cunning look on his face. "Coin of the realm, legal and tender—tender as twenty fathoms of salt water can make them."

"You fool," I whispered savagely. "Don't you realize the trouble you could get us in? Have you forgotten what they did to Esteban and Guido?"

A hurt expression filled his deep set eyes and he dropped his finger. "I didn't get my monthly check from home. What'd ya think I was gonna do—thirst to death?"

Jacques, who had been listening intently to this byplay, called the bartender over to us and gave him instructions to accept no money from the Americans. Everything was on the house.

I was truly touched.

Morgan wobbled back to his table, balancing a full glass with casual unconcern. I turned back to Jacques.

"I have been waiting a long time to ask a question, Jacques," I said a bit unsteadily. "Does she still get here just in time for her ten o'clock number?"

He nodded, examining something invisible in the bottom of his glass. But he didn't answer.

"Has she made good progress with her night school?"

Again he nodded, then slowly raised his head and directed a somber look at me. "Perhaps a little too much progress, my friend."

"What do you mean, Jacques? What's wrong?"

He shrugged, preferring to watch Henry's supple fingers flash across the piano keyboard as he answered. "Sometimes, old one, a little sophistication brings very large ambition. She is a very beautiful girl. No. More than that. A remarkably fascinating woman—intelligent, adaptable, full of the quiet mystery."

"What the devil are you trying to tell me?"

"That she still misses you greatly, my friend. You opened the doors to a new world that was never even remotely suspected by a simple little mountain girl. This was both a wonderful and a tragic thing. But your disappearance into the maw of war also left a huge black void in this new world of hers, a void that could have been bridged by one more secure, more self-confident, more adjusted to this so-called civilized world of ours."

"For God's sake, Costeau! What *are* you talking about?"

Pulling out a handkerchief, he mopped his glistening forehead and took a deep breath. "Perhaps I am making much of nothing. I don't know. But she has found new friends—in a new, smart society that is not greatly admired by true patriots."

"But that means nothing," I said, feeling my voice rise defensively. "She is too naïve to grasp the implications. She would accept such people only at face value." Abruptly I stopped. I didn't know who I was trying to convince—Costeau or myself.

"Well, my friend," he said in a flat tone. "I hope that you are right. Perhaps you are." He hoisted his drink, giving me a small smile over the top of his glass. "At any rate, in just a few moments you can talk to her and find out for yourself."

The filtered light that bathed Henry and his piano in a warm, pink luminescence slowly began to merge through the spectrum; to orange, yellow, green—and the tempo of his playing drifted ever more slowly from jazz to lazy rhythm. Through blue to indigo. His fingers geared down their pace hypnotically. A quiet, soft as a blanket, came over the audience. And, suddenly, she was there, materialized from mood and music and magic. I felt myself slide into a state of suspended animation.

Yup, it was "Mood Indigo." Low, husky, compelling—and without a trace of an accent. She had learned well.

Her glistening black hair was still a cascade of tight curls, her eyes still blue as the open sky. And she had also learned to project the very essence of her vibrant, magnetic, somehow distant personality. Again I had the feeling I was watching someone I had never really known at all, an image of an image. I was jealous—but I didn't know of what. It was futile to be jealous of time, yet that was the only thing that separated us. Or was it?

But as I watched the way she tilted back her head, watched the wondrous curves of her body stretching beneath the taunting black silk, watched the quiet smile in her eyes, I knew that Costeau had to be wrong. She was utterly incapable of pretending to be anything more than she was—a beautiful, simple girl from the hills.

With the spotlight in her eyes I didn't think she could see anyone in the quiet darkness of her audience, but the dark filter had cut down the contrast. And I was standing no more than twenty feet away. Her eyes, which had swept the room with slow, professional intimacy, suddenly stopped and stared, unbelievingly, in my direction. Her voice faltered momentarily, then quickly regaining control, rose in volume and a great, unprofessional smile wreathed her face. The sparkling dewiness that came to her eyes made me feel ten feet tall.

"You're crazy, Costeau," I muttered thickly. "Completely, absolutely crazy."

He shrugged his massive shoulders. "I have been accused of this before, my friend. But I have never before hoped it were true."

"I hope you will pardon me," I said. "But I have a sudden urgent compulsion to be elsewhere."

When I realized he hadn't answered, I managed to swing my eyes away from Tulana for a quick look at Costeau. The big Frenchman was directing a black, murderous gaze toward the entrance of the casino, his mustachios quivering with anger. The tendons of his hands rose in coarse ridges as he gripped the edge of the rail.

I turned and looked in the same direction. Everything appeared normal. A crowded throng, two or three deep, was at the bar where they could increase their drinking efficiency by being closer to the source of supply. Among them, about halfway down, I could see Morgan's head leaning over his drink. Apparently he chose to do his celebrating in solitary splendor. Then I jerked upright as I saw the object of Costeau's venomous stare. It was Sergeant Takahito.

He jostled his way through the crowd with a contemptuous swagger, rudely pushing people aside, his eyes fixed on me. A loose grin indicated he was enjoying whatever purpose there was behind his visit.

"Nip swine!" spit Costeau. "I thought I had cured them of coming here. He seems to be looking for somebody."

"Yeah," I answered with a hopeless feeling. "Me."

Costeau turned toward me in surprise. "Do you know him?"

I nodded, briefly identifying the kempe sergeant. "And I've got a feeling that he's up to no good. Sure hope he doesn't spot Morgan, or vice versa." With the amount of liquor the diver had consumed there was no telling what might happen.

Takahito had now come up within a few feet of Morgan but with his eyes intent on me he failed to notice the diver. Morgan had lifted his head and was staring vacantly in front of him. I was about to let out a sigh of relief when suddenly all hell broke loose.

Morgan obviously had been watching the approach of the burly guard in the bar mirror. As Takahito stepped behind him, he whirled around, smooth and swift as a panther, a savage snarl on his face. Before Takahito could react, Morgan hammered a pile-driver blow into his midsection, pushing every ounce of his strength and fury behind it.

Takahito was in superb physical condition. Exhaling sharply, he took a step backward. There would have been just as much reaction from a punching bag. Automatically, however, he also dropped his hands to his stomach. Morgan quickly moved forward and swung again. Traveling a vicious, whistling, two feet through the air, the punch landed directly on the blunt point of Takahito's jaw. His eyes went blank and he fell over backward, hitting the floor with a sodden thud.

The milling crowd in the casino went wild, shouting, cheering, screaming. It was like a bullfight at the moment of truth. But the mood quickly changed as Japanese guards came storming through the arched doorway. Holding their rifles crosswise, they made futile attempts to prevent the determined, surging mass from escaping through the exits. The crowd got ugly. Fistfights broke out. The guards retaliated, angrily jabbing with their gun butts. Then, preoccupied with a guard who was attempting to pin me against the bar with his gun, I heard Frank's voice rise above the melee.

"Morgan! Morgan—don't do it!"

I glanced over my shoulder to see Morgan clutching the broken neck of a beer bottle in his hand. He was turning back to the still unconscious figure of Takahito which lay on the floor, flaming rage contorting his dark features. Frank and the rest of the divers had been crowded into the alcove by an encircling ring of soldiers who now were gaining the upper hand.

I made a quick feint at the guard covering me and managed to kick his feet from under him. Morgan was dropping one knee to the reviving sergeant's chest and lifting the jagged piece of glass high in the air. After half a dozen bounds toward them, I launched myself in a flying tackle and hit Morgan across the shoulders. We rolled over, sprawling on the floor.

As I scrambled up in a sitting position, Takahito came to his feet, bellowing in maniacal fury. He jerked out his pistol.

"Now," he shouted. "You die! You die!"

Lifting the pistol, he took carefully deliberate aim between Morgan's eyes.

Suddenly a curt command was shouted out in Japanese and the nightmarish tableau was frozen in position. There was nothing but the sound of heavy breathing from the more active participants. I didn't have any breath left to breathe. At the far end of the room I could see Henry still seated at the piano. Next to it stood Tulana. She was staring in white-faced terror, a knuckle of her hand clenched in her teeth.

Through the doorway stalked a cool, aristocratic figure. It was Colonel Yamata, resplendent in his dress uniform, slapping a riding crop against the mirror-polish of his boots. He stopped in the middle of the floor and surveyed the scene with thin-lipped irritation.

"Takahito," he finally snapped. "Put away that gun before you blow off your foot."

The sergeant complied slowly, with a furiously reluctant expression plainly indicating that, at the moment, he'd just as soon shoot the Colonel as be deprived of his revenge on Morgan.

Colonel Yamata addressed me. "I am very disappointed. I had assumed that American officers were capable of better control."

I could think of no appropriate reply.

"But the party is over, anyway," he continued, contempt dripping from his voice. "Even had this unfortunate event never occurred, I have received instructions to take you back to Corregidor immediately. There is a typhoon alert—already the sea is getting very rough—and we must return to protect the equipment."

"But, Colonel," I protested lamely, "wouldn't it be better to return in the daylight tomorrow? The point of this trip was to build morale. Just the opposite has been accomplished if we must return immediately."

He shook his head with imperial hauteur. "We return immediately, Lieutenant."

He turned to the waiting soldiers and gave them instructions to take us back to the dock. Before we were herded off, his glance fell on Tulana and held there for a long moment.

"Is she with one of you?" he demanded, still staring at her.

"No," I answered. "She is an entertainer—a singer."

"Do you know her?"

"Yes."

His eyes flicked me lightly. "I am not surprised. Perhaps you would be kind enough to introduce us."

I had no choice. With frustrated anger, I stood by while he gave her a courteous and courtly bow, kissing her hand. A slant-eyed Lord Chesterfield.

"Had I but known," he smiled at her smoothly, "I would have permitted Lieutenant Sheridan to return to Manila much sooner."

Real clever the way he slipped that in. He was master-race stuff. I was just a peon on a leash.

She gave him a small, weak smile and nodded without answering. But she stared up at the tall, aristocratic officer as though mesmerized.

As we were taken from the casino and led out through the lobby to where the trucks were waiting, I heard Costeau's voice call me in a low tone. I looked around and found him partially obscured by a potted palm, beckoning urgently. I drifted toward him circumspectly.

"That information you asked me to get, old friend," he said, "about the Filipino diver who ran away."

I nodded.

"They found him shortly after—in the Pasig River. His throat had been cut."

CHAPTER SIXTEEN

The heavy trucks growled through the dark, windswept streets. From under the arching canvas canopy I could see newspapers swirling up in clouds of dust and palm trees hunching over under the onslaught of the rising storm. Under a street light I saw a small brown dog trotting along the gutter, his tail between his legs, his head down. I knew just how he felt.

Weaving slowly through the warehouse area, we came out onto the wharf and stopped. We walked out on the long dock toward "The Pig's" fishing boat, which was moored at the last berth, the wind hitting us with shrieking fury from across the open reaches of Manila Bay. The sea was roiling angrily and salt spray bit into our lips and stung our eyes. Small craft banged against the dock with booming shudders, heavy rope creaked in agony. Overhead, thick black clouds boiled across the sky like a huge smoke screen, blotting out the moon, obliterating the stars.

Colonel Yamata, directly in front of me, leaned into the gale as he approached the fishing boat. I could make out the dim figure of "The Pig" at the rail. He spoke to the Colonel, his words shredded by the wind.

"Colonel…verree dangerous…towing the barge…sea very rough…maybe take tomorrow…?"

The rest of the men clambered aboard the fishing boat and dropped into the shelter of the cabin. I hung behind to find out what was going on.

Directly behind "The Pig's" boat loomed the dark hulk of a casco similar to the one on which we had lived for the past few months. A thick line stretched from the stern of the fishing boat, dropping in a long "V" that disappeared into the water, and then rising again to reappear on either side of the trailing casco where it was fastened to the blunt prow.

Colonel Yamata shook his head curtly in answer to "The Pig's" question. "No. They must be taken out tonight. It is the order of the General."

I jerked my thumb toward the casco. "What is that for?" I asked the Colonel over the roar of the wind.

He gave an impatient shrug of his thin shoulders. "We are taking four Japanese divers back with us. They will live on this casco." He seemed quite irritated by the matter.

I was more than irritated. To put it mildly, I was real shook up.

"But, Colonel," I shouted. "The men have agreed to bring up a larger quota. There is no necessity for this sort of action. It will only lead to a very difficult situation." Grimly, I remembered the information that Costeau had just recently uncovered for me. If any pawns were to be taken, I was going to do my best to see they weren't from my side of the board.

Colonel Yamata, however, answered with what appeared to be genuine sympathy. "I am very sorry, Lieutenant. Neither I, nor the General, knew they were coming. They have been sent out on orders from Tokyo." He paused, an enigmatic expression on his bone-taut face. "I hope they do not long remain too great a threat to your security."

With this astonishing remark he wheeled and disappeared into the patrol launch moored on the opposite side of the dock. I stared after him, open-mouthed, as the guard detail followed him aboard. He had done everything but hand me his gun.

I jumped onto the bobbing deck of the fishing boat as "The Pig," muttering sullenly to himself, prepared to cast off, and dropped into the small cabin where the other men had already taken refuge from the storm. They glanced up briefly, their faces still mirroring sullen irritation at the abrupt change in plans. I didn't blame them, but there was no time for sackcloth and ashes.

"We're taking back a barge load of trouble," I told them. "Four Jap divers are on a casco tied up behind us. We're towing them out to Corregidor."

They stared at me in varying degrees of stupefaction. Except Morgan. He was asleep.

"Jumping Judas!" Swede exclaimed. "We've had it! Once those little bastards start diving they'll cut off our water for sure."

"Yah," agreed Karl with a panic-stricken look. "Ve've got to do something—quick."

Frank, who had been looking thoughtfully at the deck between his feet, lifted his head and stared at me with unshaken calmness.

"I don't get it," he said. "I thought Colonel Yamata was satisfied with the way the job was going."

"He is," I answered. "He told me that neither he nor the General knew the divers were going to be sent out until this evening."

"That's a curious way of putting it—almost as if they didn't want any more divers."

I nodded. "His tone of voice made that even plainer." Then I repeated the Colonel's last strange remark. It completely baffled them.

"What do you make of it?" Frank asked me, frowning.

"Plenty," I answered grimly. "I think our friend, the Colonel, is on a cold, calculated program of diver decimation."

I looked around at their serious, waiting faces, then continued to unravel my macabre deduction.

"You all know there were three divers on the job before you guys were brought over. According to Esteban, two were lost on the bottom under mysterious circumstances. Like Nick Borrelli was. The third diver, a Filipino, ran away. Well, I found out from Costeau tonight that that diver had been murdered and thrown in the Pasig River! Which simply means that no diver has ever learned the exact location of the silver and left the job alive." I stopped to let the implications sink in.

"But how do you know Yamata is responsible?" Frank demanded.

"I don't know for sure," I admitted, "but it fits the overall picture. Guido told me he thought Takahito killed Nick by fouling his airline, and my guess is the native divers went the same way. I think Takahito did it on instructions from Yamata. When Yamata found out that American divers were coming onto the job, he simply eliminated the first divers—and later Nick—to slow down the rate at which the silver was salvaged. And I think he is plotting with the connivance, or at least agreement, of the General."

"But what's the point?" asked Swede, with a lost look.

Karl enlightened him. "The point is—our goot friend, the Colonel, plans to come back after the war and get the silver for himself and the General."

Frank gave a short, cynical laugh. "If the General is in this with the Colonel, I wouldn't give as much for his chances as I would a snowball in hell."

The fishing boat lurched and staggered over one mountainous wave after another, interrupting our conversation as we clawed for support. We could hear the heavy line attached to the casco creak and snap taut as we slid into a valley of water with express-train speed; then it slackened for a few moments while the fishing boat panted its way up the next mountain.

During one of the lulls, Frank turned to Joe. "Say, did I see you slip a bottle of booze inside your shirt before we left the casino?"

Joe grinned. "Yeah, man. Twelve-year old scotch. Thought it might come in handy in case of snake bite."

Frank gave him a tight smile. "This time the scotch is going to fry a pig. Take it up to the captain of this luxury liner and present it to him with our compliments."

"What!" ejaculated Joe in mortal anguish.

Frank swept the rest of us with glittering and purposeful eyes. "When 'The Pig' gets so soused that he doesn't know what's going on, we're going to play pirate—and take over his ship."

"Dot's suicide," announced Karl flatly. "Ve could neffer make a run for it in this leaky tub."

"I know that," Frank answered shortly. "The patrol launch would be on our backs in no time. But we've got to do something—and fast—about those Japs on the casco."

Joe stumbled over to the ladder and scrambled his way up into the howling darkness, clutching his precious cargo against his chest.

"But vot can ve do?" asked Karl, watching Joe disappear. "Ve can't chust cut the line—the Japs vould know ve did it."

"No," Frank agreed. "It's got to look like an accident. Maybe we can fray the rope. In this heavy sea, and without power, the casco would be swamped in no time."

Swede's face was covered with a big, callous smile. "That ought to do it. No one could swim in those waves very far."

It didn't sound very positive to me. We argued about it for a while but no better solution occurred to us. I had to agree it would be impossible to get back to the casco by working our way along the line. When it snapped taut a grip of iron would have been broken.

The minutes ticked by.

"Jeez," muttered Frank. "That guy must have a stomach made of boiler plate."

We silently considered the capacity of "The Pig." If he held out long enough, we would be at Corregidor before we could take any action. The specter of a long rot in some prison camp loomed over us. Then, just as I was about to propose the calculated risk of throwing "The Pig" overboard to facilitate matters, he came lurching down the ladder. He was roaring an obscene sailors' ditty at the top of his lungs, and fell into the cabin still clutching the nearly empty bottle in his fist.

He stopped in the middle of the floor and surveyed us with rolling eyes as though surprised to find us on his boat, then lifted the bottle and poured the rest of its contents into his face. Some of it slobbered out the corner of his mouth and dribbled down his chin. Suddenly he bellowed at Karl and Frank to get off his bunk and dove at it blindly. They jumped nimbly aside and aided his forward momentum with a shove. He hit the bunk with a crash, a sigh, and a huge belch. And promptly passed out.

Swede stared at him, then picked up the empty bottle and hefted it in his hand.

"Maybe I should make sure," he suggested.

"No," I said. "He's had it. He should stay put for the rest of the trip."

"Yeah," agreed Frank. "Now, let's get going. We haven't got any time to waste."

We struggled up the ladder into the screaming violence of the rising typhoon. The wind was shrieking with insane fury, tearing the tops from the black mountains of water and exploding them into a barrage of stinging pellets. Half-blinded, we worked our way to the stern and looked for the casco. It was fifty or sixty feet behind us, almost straight down in the trough of a monstrous wave.

I edged my way back to Joe, who was fighting the wheel.

"How are you making out?" I yelled above the wind.

He forced a tired grin. "Helluva place for a guy from a tank battalion."

"I'll take over." Karl told him, coming up beside me. "Why don't you get below and watch 'The Pig'? Make sure he stays unconscious."

As Joe disappeared, I fought my way back to the stern, where Frank and Swede were staring at the casco, wondering what course of action should be taken. Morgan suddenly appeared beside us, red-eyed but wide awake. Joe apparently had given him a quick rundown on the situation.

"Look!" Morgan shouted at us, pointing to the line attached to the port side of the casco. "That side of the line is a little shorter than the other. Notice how the casco is riding off at an angle?"

He was right. It was slightly skewed to our forward course. Every time it cut through the crest of a wave, the weight of the water forced the port side dangerously deep under the surface.

"Maybe we could pull it shorter," I suggested. "If it hits a wave just right it might go under."

It wasn't very good, but lacking any better idea it was worth a try. We waited until there was a bit of slack, then all four of us got a grip on the line and pulled. It wasn't as easy as it sounded. Sweating and straining, it nearly exhausted our combined efforts to pull up a foot or two and secure it around a deck cleat. We rested until we dipped over another wave, when more slack was available, and repeated our effort. It seemed an eternity before we noticed any results. But finally the casco was beginning to yaw in widening swings. Suddenly, Swede pointed his finger and shouted.

"Hey, look! They've seen us!"

We peered into the darkness, our grips frozen to the line. On the prow of the casco we could barely make out a dim figure. It was one of the Jap divers—and he realized the danger immediately. He shouted an alarm and was joined promptly by the other three divers. We could see their white faces as they screamed at us in rage.

A desperate tug-of-war ensued. The Jap divers pulled on the longer line on the starboard side in a frantic effort to get the casco back on a straight course. We strained with even greater desperation on the port line. If the Jap divers ever got to the safety of the island and reported the incident, we wouldn't have to worry about slow rot in a prison camp—it would be quick and final.

Our hands were burned raw and bleeding, the salt spray biting into them like a million red ants. Our eyes felt like something fished out of a Mexican stew. Inch by inch, we gained the advantage. Although nearly ready to collapse from fatigue, our bigger frames and heavier weight exacted their toll.

With abrupt suddenness it was all over. A huge wall of water dropped over the casco with smothering, smashing force. The prow bit deep into the angry sea, stalling the forward progress of the fishing boat. Slowly, the stern of the casco rose, hesitated. then gradually arched over the prow in complete surrender.

Silently we watched the trailing hulk. It looked like a dead whale.

CHAPTER SEVENTEEN

The following day dawned, a transparency in blue and gold. The distant mountains and jungles of Luzon were sharply etched against the clear sky that was now washed clean of everything except a few white seagulls. They were prospecting for easy pickings in the aftermath of the storm. Along the rocky coast line of Corregidor we could see Japs busy at work—picking up debris, repairing damaged piers, pushing boats back into the water.

Idly, I watched a patrol launch moving toward us from the east side of Bataan, just a few miles distant. Frank came out and leaned on the rail beside me.

"We were lucky," he said. "The main part of the storm must have hit somewhere out in the China Sea. I hate to wish anyone bad luck, but I hope the Jap Fleet was in the middle of it."

"Amen," I answered. "I wonder how Karl and Swede made out on the PT boat last night?"

Frank glanced toward the opposite side of the dock and surveyed the gray hull with a critical eye. "Looks like it came through all right. Surprised they haven't come back by now, though. But when Karl gets on that thing you can't get him off."

The patrol launch had moved in close to shore and headed for a dock just a hundred yards or so west of us. We watched it tie up and heard the engine cut off. The sailors climbed onto the dock and turned to grasp a bulky, canvas-wrapped bundle handed up to them from the cockpit of the launch. They laid it carefully on the planking and repeated the performance. Four bundles altogether.

We pulled our eyes away and looked in another direction.

"I feel like a murderer," I muttered.

"Yeah," Frank quietly agreed. "But dead men tell no tales."

The next morning we returned to the familiar routine—but with a surprising change. Dropping from the casco into the fishing boat, we were met by a young Filipino who was wearing a brilliant embroidered shirt and an ear-to-ear grin.

We couldn't help staring. Little things loomed large in our current lives.

"Who are you?" I asked the grin.

"Hernando, *señor.*" His white teeth flashed at us as he gunned the engine. "I am the brother of Rosita."

It took a moment for me to recall that Rosita was the maid at Colonel Yamata's cottage—and the widow of a diver.

"Where is 'The Pig'?"

"*Perdone usted?*"

"The fat character who has been ..."

"Oh," he interrupted, his smile even broader. "The Japs, they put him in prison. They said he was responsible for the deaths of four divers. My sister heard this from Colonel Yamata last night. She told him that I am the best pilot in the world, so I was given the job this morning. Now I take you to the diving barge."

His sister's opinion of Hernando's proficiency may have been colored by a bit of bias, but what he lacked in accuracy he more than made up with speed and guts. In no time we rounded the point and bore down on the barge, like a B-17 coming in for a strafing run. As we clutched for support, he skidded around the stern in a tight circle and reversed the engine just before we plowed into the hull of the barge. We back-watered frantically, then touched alongside with the gentlest of bumps. Gratefully, we escaped onto the deck of the barge.

"Gott!" Karl was ashen-faced. "A born PT boat pilot!"

The first dives of the day were made by Frank and Swede, who went to the bottom around the middle of the afternoon. In spite of reassuring answers, we began to grow worried as their allotted time under water stretched out beyond the safety limit.

"Nearly ten minutes overdue," muttered Karl, with a shake of his head. "I don't underschtand."

I didn't, either. Usually the divers cut their time as short as possible in accordance with our conservation policy. But Frank and Swede had even sent up two extra boxes of silver.

"Maybe they don't know how long they've been down," I suggested.

"They know. They've acknowledged my signal to come up. No, something iss cooking." Karl leaned over the rail and stared into the water as though he could see the two men. Suddenly he stood up with a satisfied grunt as the line jerked in his hands. "Ach. There they are. Now they are coming up."

We waited impatiently through the slow stages of the decompression routine. Finally they burst through the surface and clambered aboard.

"For Chrissake," I growled at Frank, as I removed his helmet, "what were you trying to do—give us heart failure? And what was the idea of the two extra boxes of silver? We're a little short of Congressional medals of honor."

He rubbed his hands together and grinned at us. "That was just a cover-up in case our extra time on the bottom was noticed. Swede and I hit pay dirt. That big scrap pile down there got shifted around during the storm. Spread out all over the place. We were poking around, trying to find more ammunition for our automatics. And—guess what we found!" He leaned forward and dropped his voice. "A propeller for the PT boat—brand new—in perfect condition!"

We gaped unbelievingly. Karl found his voice first.

"How do you know it vill fit?"

"It says so, right on the crate," Swede answered. "Stenciled in nice, big, black letters."

Apparently sensing our excitement, Sergeant Takahito started to move toward us, sullen and suspicious. We broke off our conversation and returned to work with soaring spirits. Frank helped Karl and Morgan with their helmets, giving them quick instructions to find the propeller and take it to the descending line.

"We've got to take a calculated risk with Hernando," he said in a low voice. "We can't get the propeller back to the casco without his help."

"I think he's safe," I answered, helping Karl over the rail. "What do you want him to do?"

He leaned next to me and watched the bubbles rising from the submerging divers. "Ask him to bring about a hundred and twenty feet of new line with him tomorrow. When he ties up next to the diving barge in the afternoon he is to fasten one end to his boat and drop the other end over the side with a small weight attached. We'll tie on the propeller and he can pull it up where it'll ride under the keel. We can cut it loose when we get back to the casco."

I nodded and leaned my back against the rail, noting with surprise that none of the guards was anywhere in sight. Not even the stolid sergeant. Then Colonel Yamata hove into view on the upper deck, blinking in the brilliant sunlight. He nodded at us with a smile cold enough to solidify water.

"Lieutenant," he said suavely, "I have just been advised by Sergeant Takahito that you have delivered a bonus of two extra boxes of silver today. Without going into your motives for this commendable endeavor, I wish to reward you with a few cold bottles of beer which you will find in the galley."

The Colonel withdrew into the shade of his awning. Frank and I looked at each other and promptly turned toward the galley, assuring Swede we would be back in a couple of minutes to relieve him at the air compressor.

The Jap cook jerked his thumb toward the refrigerator. I pulled out two bottles, snapped off the caps, and handed one to Frank. We held them up in a silent toast to the day's good fortune. Our heads tilted back, we were savoring our unexpected treat in full measure—and then abruptly froze as a bellow of panic came from the stern. It was Swede.

"Jim! Frank!"

Our bottles crashed to the table in unison and we raced out onto the open deck. Swede was still at the compressor, his face contorted with hate and rage, and his eyes following Sergeant Takahito who was just disappearing around the superstructure on the port side.

"That bastard just cut Morgan's air hose with a meat cleaver," Swede choked out. "Did it before I even knew he was here. Take the compressor, will you? I'm going to kill the sonuvabitch!"

I took the pump handle automatically and Swede lunged across the deck in pursuit of Takahito. Frank never broke his stride as he heard Swede's words. He went over the stern rail with a high leap in a desperate effort to catch the severed end of Morgan's air hose. Takahito reappeared from the port side, screaming for help, Swede in grim pursuit slashing at him with his huge fists. From the bow, several guards pounded toward the confused scene of action. Colonel Yamata came to the upper-deck rail but his shouted commands went unheard and unheeded.

Swede trapped Takahito against the stern rail and beat him with untiring, triphammer blows. Two guards jumped on his back. He paid no attention to them until Takahito slid to the deck, his face a wet, crimson mask, then he pulled them around and flung them at the bulkhead like sacks of wheat. Two more guards rushed up with drawn revolvers. Swede took a quick look, realized he could no longer cope with the entire pack and picked up Takahito by an arm and a leg and threw him overboard. He landed fifteen feet from the barge with a geyser-like splash. A snapped order from Colonel Yamata sent two guards over the rail to his aid.

Frank came up the ladder, gasping and choking for breath. He had been under for an interminable period of time. He shook his head.

"My God!" I said. "What do we do now?"

"Nothing we can do," he panted, "except pull him up, put another hose on his helmet, and send him back down again so he can decompress."

Swede came up to us heaving for breath. Frank looked at him in surprise, obviously wondering what had happened. But there was no time for questions. Working as rapidly as possible, Swede started to pull up Morgan while Frank got an air hose ready. I stayed at the pump, pushing air down to Karl, who, I realized, could do nothing for Morgan. Unless they had stayed quite close together on the bottom, he would be completely unaware of the situation.

Takahito's still unconscious body was dragged aboard and carried forward. Two guards stayed behind to keep an eye on us. Colonel Yamata silently watched from the upper rail.

The few moments it took Swede to pull Morgan up from the bottom seemed like hours, and when he came over the side he was writhing in agony. It was all Frank and Swede could do to hold him still long enough to attach a replacement air hose and get him back under water. His face was blue and hideously contorted as he struggled to pull air into his starved lungs. He paid no attention to the entreaties of the men trying to help him.

"Deaf," Frank said. "He can't hear a thing."

"Permanent?" I asked.

He shrugged. "God only knows. Can't tell until we bring him up again. At least he doesn't have any water in his lungs."

Only a very short time had elapsed before they got Morgan back into the water but his fight for life seemed to have lasted an eternity. Karl, meanwhile, had started his long ascent to the surface.

There was nothing to do but wait. Limp with fatigue and nervous strain, Swede and I leaned against the rail as Frank took a turn at the compressor. Perspiration ran from us in tiny, burning rivers, saturating our clothing. I could even feel it in my shoes.

I lit a cigarette with fingers that trembled violently. Like a pianist playing an invisible piano.

"What do you think his chances are?" I asked Swede in a voice that accompanied my fingers.

He shrugged his thick shoulders. "It's impossible to say. Putting him back down will force the nitrogen back into solution with his body fluids. If we bring him up real slow he could be O.K. At this depth, though, it'd be a miracle. He might live—and he might not."

I shuddered involuntarily. The horrible feeling hit me that even if Morgan did live he might wish he hadn't.

Karl finally came to the surface and we pulled him aboard. Quickly telling him what had happened, we asked how Morgan had looked when he passed him on his way up. Karl shook his head, still stunned at the turn of events.

"Not so goot. He isn't in great pain—but his arms and legs—he can't seem to get them straightened out."

We kept Morgan down until it was decided that any additional time would be useless. Slowly, Swede began to bring him up. Colonel Yamata called me over to tell me he had radioed for a launch to take Morgan to the Navy hospital at Cavite, which was equipped with a recompression chamber. I listened in silence, then turned away without a word. I didn't trust myself to speak.

The launch arrived within ten minutes. Morgan was brought aboard, strapped to a stretcher and, without having spoken a word, was transferred to the launch. It roared off across the pale green sea, trailing a frothy wake.

He never returned.

Takahito had made a double score. He had avenged himself for the beating administered by Morgan—and he had removed one more pawn for the Colonel in his deadly game.

CHAPTER EIGHTEEN

The next morning Hernando roared up to the casco, skidding his boat in at a forty-five degree angle behind a surging pile of waves. Ignoring our grim faces, he gave us a gleeful smile of conspiracy and pointed to a coil of new line pushed back under a seat.

"I have done just as you asked," he announced proudly, "and brought the big rope with me. It is even bigger than you asked, a hundred and fifty feet long. All through the night I have soaked it in a barrel of water so it will sink to the bottom quickly."

"Nice going, Hernando," I commended. "Be very careful when you drop it in the bay. It would be a very serious thing if you were caught by the guards."

The day passed in routine fashion, and, except for a few brief checks from the upper deck, Colonel Yamata confined himself to his cabin. This was unusual and I was more certain than ever that his magnanimous hand-out of cold beer on the previous day was related to Sergeant Takahito's meat-cleaver attack on Morgan's air hose. It also removed any lingering doubts on the part of the divers that the insane plot was more than a figment of my imagination. We felt as secure as a bunch of white mice tossed into the cage of a hungry rattlesnake.

Early in the afternoon Hernando pulled up in the fishing boat, coming in quietly to avoid attracting attention. Keeping an eye on the dozing guard, I nodded to Hernando and he dropped the line into the water and ran it down quickly. Frank and Karl, down for their last dive of the day, secured the propeller to the line. Hernando gave me a grin, indicating he had received their signal, and proceeded to pull it up while watching me for signs of alarm. But our guard merely scratched himself contentedly and slept on.

We returned to the casco without incident. After we disembarked, I turned and watched Hernando swing his boat around and start off with a roar. Just as he got to the end of the dock, he leaned over the carburetor. Instantly the engine sputtered, throbbed again to full life, then died with a tired sigh. I held my breath as the patrol launch swung around and came toward him. If one of the sharp-eyed guards spotted the line dangling stiffly into the water, suspending its precious burden, no amount of fast talk was going to save our equally precious hides.

Hernando stood up and waved them off, shouting that it was only a minor adjustment and he would soon have it fixed. The launch throttled down to a crawl, however, and turned in slow circles a few yards off the port side of the fishing boat. It was obvious they intended to wait until he was on his way to Manila.

Frank spoke in soft, imploring tones from the doorway behind me. "Cut it loose, Hernando! Cut it loose!"

"We'll never get it back if he does," I said grimly. "He's past the drop-off. It's thirty or forty feet deep out there."

By now we could see that an argument had developed in the patrol launch. Two of the guards were jabbering excitedly as they stabbed their fingers toward Hernando, apparently making the point that they should move in closer. Another guard was pointing in the direction of Manila and shouting with equal determination. His lone voice was louder than the other two put together.

The hassle went on for several moments while we watched tensely, then, to our vast relief, the launch headed off across the bay at top speed.

Frank gave a heartfelt sigh. "Must be going off duty," he said weakly.

Hernando stood up and watched the launch roar across the water. Turning toward us, he pointed at his carburetor with a forlorn shrug.

"Great!" Frank exclaimed. "Now he's got it so fouled up he can't get it started."

The current was sweeping him around the dock, however, in the general direction of the PT boat. The guards from the upper end of the dock came out and watched for a while, shouting advice in Japanese, which meant very little to Hernando. It was ribaldly useless, anyway. Finally they tired of the game and returned to their shack.

It was nearly dark before Hernando floated in close enough to lasso one of the pilings with a long, impossibly lucky cast. He pulled the boat in with the air of one who did these things every day and soon had snuggled up directly behind the PT boat.

We ate supper while we waited for the complete darkness of night. Swede and Karl, anticipating a considerable amount of time in the water while mounting the propeller, had only a sandwich and a cup of tea.

"How much more work is there to be done," I asked Karl, "before she's ready to go?"

"Just the propeller," he said. "Everything else I haff checked a dozen times. I can do no more. It is impossible to know vot is going to happen vithout turning over the engines."

"It'll be a big gamble," Frank interposed. "Like Russian roulette—we'll either be on our way, or we'll be dead."

Swede and Karl had stripped down to their shorts. We followed them out onto the stern and watched as they silently slipped over the rail and swam under the pier toward Hernando's boat. The faint splashes they made seemed to boom like cannon in the quiet of the night and we cringed each time, praying the guards wouldn't come galloping down the dock to investigate.

Joe Price came out carrying a cardboard box under his arm. He held it up.

"Pies," he explained. "One for the Colonel—and two for the guards to keep them busy for a while."

"Attaboy, Joe!" I said. "Too bad you didn't have a few sleeping pills to put in them."

"Well," Frank murmured, stoking up his pipe, "It won't be long now."

I nodded. "It won't be too tough leaving our island paradise, but I hate to think of all that silver being left for the Japs."

Frank grunted. "Don't worry about that. We've got ninety per cent of it hidden in that cave you saw. We blocked up the entrance with boulders. They couldn't find it even if they were leaning against the front entrance."

We spent another hour in idle conversation before Karl and Swede rose silently up the side of the casco and pulled themselves aboard.

"Judas!" Frank exclaimed, startled. "You two make a great pair of pirates. Did you get the job done?"

"You bet!" Swede grinned. "The propeller slipped right into place. She's ready to go!"

Karl was a bit more cautious. "The nut that holds it in place went on a little too easy. The thread is worn and I couldn't pull it up as tight as it should be. I'll double check it tomorrow."

"Where is Hernando?" I asked. "Hasn't he got his carburetor fixed yet?"

"No," Swede answered. "We took a look at it, but it's too dark to see what's wrong. He's going to sleep on his boat tonight and we'll fix it in the morning."

We went back into the casco, where Swede and Karl rubbed down and put on dry clothes. Deciding that a celebration was in order, I consulted our stock, selected two bottles of sparkling burgundy and stood them in a pail. Then I dumped all the ice cubes from the refrigerator around them and rotated the bottles with a professional twist.

The fact began to register that we were actually about ready to gamble for escape. Everyone was talking at once, saying things we had already said several times. Then abruptly our voices stilled. The sound of frantically flying feet reverberated on the wooden planks of the dock, like a drumbeat heralding the day of doom.

"It's Joe." Tension strained Swede's voice. "Running like all the banshees in hell was after him."

We heard him hit the stern of the casco with a flying leap. Immediately he burst in, his face drawn and white, his breath coming in short, ragged gasps. Collapsing on the edge of the nearest cot, he tried to speak but in his desperate urgency broke into a coughing spell that racked him to the soles of his shoes.

"Take it easy, Joe," Frank cautioned. "Take your time."

Joe looked up at the circle of alarmed faces crowded around him. With a tremendous effort at self-control, he took a deep breath and pulled himself together.

"All hell has busted loose!" he choked in a gravelly voice. "They're coming to get us. We've got to get out of here fast. I hope you guys got the boat ready."

He paused, panting for breath. Frank spoke up in a soothing voice. "Calm down and just take it easy. Start at the beginning and tell us what's wrong."

Joe shook his head impatiently, but managed to become a little more coherent.

"While I was talking to Rosita," he said, "the captain of the guard came to Colonel Yamata's cottage with a bunch of soldiers. I hid in the bushes out in back while Rosita went inside to find out what was going on. She came back in a couple of minutes and told me that the Japs had traced those pesos that Esteban and Guido gave to the junk dealer so he would hold the propeller for them."

"Well," Frank shrugged, "that's not so serious. The Japs already knew Esteban and Guido had some of the silver. Besides, it's all over Manila anyway."

Joe shook his head violently. "Let me finish. They also found out what the money was for—a propeller for the PT boat!"

The impact of his words froze us to the spot. Frank broke loose first, whirling toward our cache of automatics and ammunition.

"Let's go!" he shouted. "This is it!"

We exploded into action. Grim-faced, almost wordlessly, we snatched up the first things that occurred to us. Swede and Joe threw food into two burlap bags. I helped Frank with the guns. Karl grabbed an armful of blankets.

Within two or three minutes we piled out into the darkness of night on the stern of the casco and took a quick look toward the guard shack. One of the guards had just stepped out to snap on the floodlights that bathed the upper end of the pier in a hot pool of illumination. He leaned against the shack, his back toward us, and a match flared briefly as he lit a cigarette. Frank edged up onto the rail and trained one of the automatics on him.

"O.K.," he said tersely. "One at a time. Take off your shoes— and make it fast."

Joe hunched over and scuttled across the dock. Then Karl. I looked around for Swede and found he had disappeared back into the casco. I stuck my head inside and found him coming toward me, the bucket of champagne clenched in one free finger.

"Necessary," he answered my unspoken question. "We ain't got water."

I followed him across with Frank right at my heels. As I climbed onto the PT boat, Hernando materialized from the shadows and began stowing away the equipment we had brought along. Even in the darkness his white teeth flashed in a big grin of excitement. He looked about as worried as a Texas oil millionaire who had just won the Irish sweepstakes.

Working furiously against time, we cut loose the lines and pushed against the pilings to swing the boat free. With excruciating slowness the dark strip of water between us and the dock gradually widened. At last the stern of the PT boat was out far enough so we could reverse the engines and back out without hitting Hernando's fishing boat. Joe left us and ran up to the starboard gun mount and started ripping off the canvas cover. Swede disappeared below to get the ammunition belts. Karl turned to Hernando.

"Take the wheel," he ordered tautly. "You're going to be our pilot."

I could sense, rather than see, Karl's hands shaking as he went over to the starter button. I didn't blame him. I was shaking all over. He took a deep breath and looked around at us.

"Vell, men," he announced nervously, "here goes nothing."

"For Chrissake, hurry," Frank shouted from the rail. "Here comes our farewell party!"

CHAPTER NINETEEN

unging across the deck to Frank's side, I slipped off the safety
catch on my automatic. Toward the upper end of the dock,
Jap soldiers were pouring out onto the wooden planking like a
pack of hungry wolves after snowbound lambs.

"Good God!" I said. "They didn't have that many to take
Corregidor in the first place."

"Well," Frank snapped, taking careful aim, "let's start reducing the odds."

Simultaneous with the crack of his automatic, the powerful engines of the PT boat burst into a deep roar that reverberated in the warm summer night like a bomb. The soldiers,
intent on the casco, suddenly stopped in alarm—all except
one. Flinging his arms out wide, he spun halfway around and
fell backward into blackness. The rest panicked momentarily,
those in the lead piling up against the surging mass behind
them in a frantic effort to move back. Futile orders were
screamed by the captain of the guard, who followed securely
in the rear.

Then, as suddenly as it had started, the PT boat choked and
sputtered into silence. Karl literally dove through the hatch into
the engine room.

Frank and I kept up a steady stream of fire at the soldiers. The
captain had finally managed to berate them into a semblance of
a firing line, with those in front dropping to one knee so those in
the rear could fire over their heads.

Frank turned a strained face in the direction Karl had disappeared. "What the hell is he doing so long? We can't hold out for more than a minute or two."

My throat felt tight as I answered. "Something wrong with a fuel line. Got a kink in it or something."

"A kink in it?" he echoed angrily. "He's been checking out this damned boat for three months!"

We both knew Karl was not to blame. I shook my head without answering. I was too busy ducking the rifle bullets that began to whine viciously over our heads. A quick scurrying of boots sounded on the dock. Frank gave me a drawn look.

"They're moving up," he said, flatly. "We've had it!"

My answer was drowned out by a violent, staccato burst of fire that suddenly shook the PT boat from stem to stern.

"A machine gun!" Frank groaned.

"Yeah. Ours! Look up there." I pointed up at the domeless turret mount where Joe had swung the twin .50 caliber guns around and gone into action. Mixed with the short, explosive burst we could hear the screams of the Jap soldiers. We jumped up and looked over the rail. They were crumpling with grotesque finality, like a field of wheat before a huge, invisible scythe.

"*Banzai!*" Frank shouted happily.

I emptied my automatic into the melee and then sat down to load another clip. Karl popped up through the hatch from the engine room.

"Giff it another try," he ordered Hernando. "I think it's O.K. now."

"It'd better be!" Frank's voice was grim. "I hear trucks coming down the road. They're bringing up reinforcements."

Hernando gave the starter another push. The huge engines coughed, hesitated, then rose in a deep, full-throated roar. With a triumphant shout of "*Viva libertad!*" he revved them up; the propellers clawed into the water and our sleek boat backed out from the dock in a wide, sweeping curve. We cheered like a bunch of pirates who had just captured a Spanish plate ship.

It was a short-lived cheer. The Japs parked their trucks so their headlights illuminated our position as bright as day and were pouring a driving hail of bullets at us with light machine guns. I saw Hernando's shirt sleeve flutter and a dark blotch appeared, enlarging rapidly. He gave no indication that he felt it. Careening the ship over on its side as he gathered speed, he spun the wheel sharply to port, then looped around hard to starboard in violent evasive action. Sheets of water spewed from under the hull and the engines snarled their protest.

We were still headed in the general direction of Manila. Frank rushed over to Hernando and jerked him around roughly. "Where the hell are you going?" he demanded in harsh tones. "Head her out to open sea, *muy pronto!*"

Hernando winced at the grip on his wounded arm and looked around for me. I removed Frank's hand and translated his request into Spanish, at the same time giving the arm a quick check. The wound was superficial, barely breaking the skin.

Hernando answered quickly and I gave it back to Frank in English. "He says we can't get through between Corregidor and Bataan The Japs have several patrol boats in the channel because many prisoners have tried to escape by swimming across. We'll have to circle around Corregidor and go through where there is more room to maneuver."

Karl, coming up to us wiping grease from his hands, heard the translation.

"Yah," he agreed. "Ve must depend on our element of surprise. Vith only two props vorking, ve can make only thirty-five or forty knots. Better to avoid trouble in the first place than try to outrun it."

We sped around the long, crescent-shaped tail of Corregidor and headed into Caballo Bay, listening uneasily to the distant rumbling of patrol boats. They were warming up for the chase. Searchlights flashed on along the shoreline and probing fingers of light penciled across the riffled water of the bay. A warning siren set up a dismal wail.

"Can't we make any more speed?" Frank demanded of Karl. "If we don't make it out into the China Sea, in a few minutes they'll cut us off."

Karl shook his head. "She's doing the best she can. Just pray they don't spot our location in the darkness."

From our starboard side we heard the sound of an approaching patrol boat pulling out from the island in an attempt to intercept us. We listened tensely while it roared closer, but they had started too late. The PT boat's engines had warmed to peak performance and we relaxed as they fell behind, wallowing ineffectually in our wake. Hernando laughed, looking back at them. He was as happy as a kid with a shiny, new bicycle.

Suddenly, a brilliant shaft of light came from the blackness just off our bow, blinding us with its white glare. Hernando spun the wheel madly in a desperate effort to avoid a collision.

"It's the floodlight from the diving barge," Frank bellowed. "Knock it out—fast—before the shore batteries spot us."

Joe Price was scrambling back to the machine gun turret even before Frank had finished speaking. Swinging the guns around, he poured a burst at the tattletale light. The speed of our boat threw him off and the volley carried several yards ahead of the barge. He swore fluently and feelingly. Hernando swung in closer to give him a better shot. A scattering of rifle fire greeted us, and Joe spun away from the machine guns, clutching at his side.

I rushed up into the turret to bring Joe down. In unreasoning anger, I lifted my automatic and emptied the clip in the direction of the diving barge. To my amazement, the spotlight shattered into darkness, plunging us once more into the illusion of security.

I lifted Joe out of the turret and Frank promptly took his place. He barely had time to rake the barge with a long burst before we left it bobbing in the heavy swells of our wake. I lugged Joe down into the cabin and rolled him onto a bunk, then broke open a first-aid kit. He groaned feebly and I could hear the grating of his teeth as he fought against the pain. I pulled up his shirt, exposing the wounded side. He rolled his head back and stared at me with glassy eyes.

"Is it bad, doc?"

I shook my head, unable to answer. I dusted sulfa powder over the wound while he closed his eyes for a moment. Then he opened them again and managed a feeble grin.

"Know something, doc?" His voice was so weak I had to lean over to hear clearly. "You'd better go back to med school."

"Why?" I asked, busy folding a bandage.

"Because you're plugging up the wrong hole!"

Aghast, I stared at him as he pulled his head up. His throat muscles worked spasmodically in an effort to speak, then he fell back and relaxed with a quiet sigh. I grabbed his dangling hand and felt for a pulse. There was none. Mechanically I pulled away the rest of his shirt. There was a bullet hole almost dead center in his chest.

I stumbled unseeingly up onto the deck and answered Frank's look with a shake of my head.

"Sonuvabitch!" he swore softly.

By now the shore batteries had located our general position and, divining our objective, were pouring out a broad pattern of shells along our course. Occasionally, one would hit close enough to splash water up over the deck in spite of Hernando's twisting maneuvers. In a few minutes we would put Corregidor and its flashing guns off our stern.

Suddenly, the dim outlines of a small patrol boat appeared directly in front of us. Apparently they had guessed our escape course and set out early enough to lie in wait, taking a chance that we would come close enough to effect an ambush. It was a foolhardy mistake.

Hernando took a hard grip on the wheel and held to his course, pulling his lips back in a deadly grimace. We hit the patrol boat with a violent impact. It split apart in a twisted, splintered mass of wreckage. We could hear the screams from the water on either side as we bore on.

Karl swore unhappily and told me to warn Hernando against repeating the stunt.

"If our props hit anything they could be ripped off," he muttered. "And this boat don't go fast vithout propellers."

I started to relay this advice to Hernando, but he suddenly interrupted, pointing an arm straight ahead.

"señor, look!" he shouted. "What shall I do?"

The huge dark shape of a Jap cruiser was bearing down on us. Then, on either side of the big ship we spotted the sleek outline of a destroyer. They were moving fast.

Frank cursed with long, low violence and I found myself joining him with equal fervor. Swede just looked at the ships, his shoulders sagging hopelessly.

"Probably just coming in from a routine patrol," he said softly. "Of all the damned, dumb, stupid luck!"

"Ve can't possibly get by them," Karl said. "At the speed ve're making those destroyers could easily outrun us. They're no doubt looking for us anyvay. By this time they vould have been varned by radio."

"We'd better figure out something in a helluva hurry," I said, "before we drive right up their gun barrels. If we can't get out into the China Sea, we'll have to go as far north as possible up Manila Bay."

Frank gave me a discouraged look. "It's the only thing we can do. But we'll need a damn sight more luck than we've had so far to cross overland to the mountains in northern Luzon without getting caught."

Hernando wheeled the boat around and we started to retrace our course back across Caballo Bay.

"We may still have a good chance, *señor*," he said, still managing a smile. "I have friends at the north end of the bay at Malolos. They will help us."

I tried to return his smile. "Right at the moment there's nothing we need like friends."

Our reversing maneuver had caught the Jap patrol off guard, for they had spread out and reduced speed, waiting for us to come within range. By the time we had crossed Caballo Bay, however, one of the destroyers had picked up speed and was in hot pursuit. We could barely make out her location against the lighter sky as she began to close the gap, which at the moment was four or five miles wide.

As we raced northward, now opposite the dim glow of Manila, a large, fast launch arched out to intercept us from the east. When they came in to close range we could see several dim figures lining the rail.

"Tell Hernando to get on her stern," Frank shouted at me as he rushed for the gun turret. "They've got a machine gun mounted on the bow!"

Hernando swerved in behind the launch. Although they could make better speed than we, our attack apparently unnerved them. They must have figured we would try to outrun them. They tried to pull away from us and Frank gave the launch a long, raking burst from the twin machine guns. The heads disappeared below the rail and the launch, now out of control, lost power as we came alongside. From our higher vantage point we poured a heavy fire into them, Frank with the machine guns, Swede and I with our automatics. We roared on, leaving the launch behind— a riddled, lifeless hulk.

"That does it," Frank announced. "We're out of ammo for the machine guns."

We turned to look for the destroyer. It was less than two miles behind us. This was going to be a great fight: .45 automatics against the guns of a Mutsuki-class warship.

Their first shell hit no more than twenty yards off our stern. Frank glanced at me, his lips tightly compressed significantly. This was the kind of shooting that needed no comment. Hernando, fearing to lose any more ground by evasive action, headed directly for the black jungle of Bataan that filled the skyline on our left. With our shallower draft we might be able to scoot along the shoreline while the destroyer would be forced to stand off farther out in the bay.

The maneuver gained us several hundred precious yards. The destroyer seemed to hesitate momentarily as they started to follow us in toward the coast. Then it swung out and put on speed, attempting to pull up parallel where they could pin us down with shell fire. In a few minutes they pulled out all the stops, laying down a murderous barrage of shells that splashed all around us.

"We can't make it," Frank shouted. "We'll have to take our chances in the jungle. Tell Hernando to hit the beach."

The PT boat started to rock from the concussion of near misses. I clawed my way up to Hernando and shouted instructions at him to head for shore. He nodded as calmly as if he were out on a Sunday drive in the family car. Spinning the wheel hard to port, he headed the prow directly at the beach which was a bare hundred yards away.

I had just started back when a shell hit the stern with a shattering explosion. A bulkhead swung down and hammered me on the head as we tilted up on our side. Pulling myself upright, I saw Karl lying on the deck. He was groaning and pulling his legs up to his belly. Swede had disappeared.

"Jim!" I heard Frank shout. "Tell Hernando to get out. We've got to swim for it."

I saw him jump up onto the rail, preparing to dive. I turned to shout at Hernando, but he was already stumbling toward me. With a beckoning wave at him to hurry, I turned and headed for the rail. Before I reached it, a shell hit the PT boat directly amidships. It disintegrated with a scream of protest. Debris flew through the air like huge pieces of shrapnel. Something hit me with stunning force and I felt myself driven deep under water. Deep into warm blackness.

CHAPTER TWENTY

After an eternity, I fought my way back to the surface. It was twenty thousand leagues of giddy nausea. A millenium of thunderous pain. In the wet, cloying blackness I seized onto something solid and raised a weak arm to feel the aching lump between my ears. It was a head. Apparently mine. Then came a rhythmic sloshing of shallow water, accompanied by an alarmed voice. It was Frank.

"Jim! Is that you?"

"Yeah," I croaked. "Where are the others?"

He leaned over in the darkness and pulled me up off the boulder that I had been hugging.

"Are you O.K.?" he demanded, ignoring my question.

"Yeah, yeah. Something clobbered me in the back. Just knocked the wind out of me." As we talked, another figure splashed toward us from the dense underbrush along the shore. It was Swede. He spoke with great relief in his voice.

"Thank God! I thought I was the only one left."

"You didn't see either Karl or Hernando?" I asked.

Swede shook his head.

"Neither did I," Frank spoke up grimly, "and I've been scouring all around these damned rocks. Either they're already into the jungle or ..." He let the sentence die unfinished.

Although we searched for them everywhere we turned up no clue in the fate of either Karl or Hernando. After twenty minutes of stumbling up and down the rocky shoreline in the darkness we were forced to abandon our efforts when the destroyer lowered a landing party which sped toward us in implacable pursuit. Wearily, we pushed inland, heading instinctively toward the protection of the rugged hills that formed the backbone of the Bataan Peninsula.

It took us nearly two weeks to work our way north along the craggy ridges, keeping our course generally in the direction of Bontoc which still remained our immediate objective. After that we were somewhat vague, but it seemed that the mountains of northern Luzon, where we had heard that guerilla bands were forming, would be our best bet.

Our luck stayed with us. Although we occasionally saw Jap military convoys on the roads below us, we were never spotted. We even had a brief skirmish with a small four-man patrol that was taking time out for a swim in a mountain stream. Since we had their guns before they could get out of the water, the whole show was over in a couple of minutes. We wolfed down their rations, confiscated their rifles, and continued on our way without a backward glance.

As we left the protective cover of the mountains, however, and dropped down to the central plain of Luzon, the going became rougher. There was more activity of all sorts—military and civilian—and we found that we could travel safely only at night. With the aid of sympathetic Filipinos, to whom we were forced to turn when the food situation became critical, we eventually found our way to Bontoc and the plantation of Señor Mendez who was the father of Carlotta, Frank's playmate of prewar days.

It was Nirvana, Paradise, and Lost Horizon all rolled into one. For several months we stayed back in the wild reaches of the Mendez sugar estate luxuriating in our freedom. Food was brought to us by the plantation hands and there were blooded horses to ride across our thirty-thousand-acre kingdom. Then it came to an abrupt and jarring end.

Swede, who was a particularly restless sort, had taken to riding further afield every day, looking for something on which to expend his limitless energy. Ultimately, he found a small, native village tucked away on some unmapped crossroads.

"Come on," he urged Frank and me as he swung up into the saddle. "They've got a poolroom, beer—and *señoritas* who're crazy about Americans!"

"Not on your tintype," I answered. "And you'd better stay away, too, Swede. There's a reward for turning in Americans to the Jap military."

"Hell," he laughed, "I been there every day for two weeks. Nobody'd turn me in or they'd a done it by now. Just trying to let you guys in on a good thing!" Without waiting for further admonishing from us, he wheeled his horse around and pounded down the hill. We watched him go, wondering if we were being over-cautious.

"Bet the beer is warm," muttered Frank disconsolately.

"Yeah," I sighed. "And the *señoritas* cold."

The Japs got Swede that night. His informer got ten dollars cash. The next day we left for the mountains in the northern part of Luzon.

A month later we joined the guerilla army and, although they were the sorriest looking lot we had ever seen, it gave us a bigger thrill than when Uncle Sam had blown the bugle in the first place. Lieutenant Colonel Killian was in charge. He was a slat-thin character with cadaverous cheeks, a curt disposition, and a heart of chrome steel. His "boys"—a mixture of American soldiers, sailors and Filipino natives—had been honed into a razor-sharp, tough little organization that traveled fast, struck hard, and never took a prisoner. By comparison, our previous military experience resembled maneuvers on the drill fields of West Point or Annapolis.

Japanese efforts to exterminate us grew more determined as the months went by. With every supply train blown up, every truck convoy shot to bits, every bridge booby-trapped, the little green men were forced into offensive action. But our grapevine never failed us. Either we were gone—or we were waiting for them. Once we were waiting for them when they returned, dog-weary, to their own camp after a futile day of beating the mountain canyons looking for us. We burned out three machine guns in the heat of the action, and never lost a man. Even "Chrome Steel" Killian smiled that night.

And it went on. Month after month. Occasionally, some of us didn't make it back. Now and then a replacement showed up—a gaunt escapee from a prison camp, or a native Filipino who'd lost his farm, his cows, or his wife to the Japs. We quit thinking in terms of weeks or months. It was the rainy season or the dry season or the typhoon season. It was '42, or '43, or '44. It went on. The eternity of war.

Then, in April of '45, we decided to hit the munition dump at Appari. We had been arguing about the risks for weeks but we all knew secretly that it had to be done. It was far bigger than anything we had tried before. We should have had ten times the number of men to remove it from the suicide category. But if we were to carry on we needed new guns, ammunition, grenades—and, more urgently, medicine and clothing.

Frank came over to my shack that night, his eternal pipe sputtering and reeking. I was afraid to ask him what he was burning in it these days.

"What's your assignment for tomorrow, Jim?" He dropped onto my bunk and groped under it with one hand.

"Diversionary," I answered. "I'm supposed to take six of the men and swing around behind their camp to make the initial assault. And if you're after my whiskey, I hid it under the pillow."

He grunted as he dragged it out and examined it against the light of the lantern. "Cripes! What are all those little chunks floating in it?"

"Protein matter. If you don't need protein you can just put the bottle back under the pillow."

I watched as he tilted it into the air and took a hefty swallow. Frank wasn't much of a drinker.

"What's yours?" I asked.

"My what?"

"Your assignment, damn it. What else are we talking about?"

"Frontal," he answered shortly. Then after another swallow, added: "You'd better make a mighty big ruckus at their back door, my friend. I've only got seventeen men left to slip in and do the dastardly deed."

He was worried. It was the first time since I'd known Frank that I'd ever heard his voice so taut, so troubled. Almost as if he had some premonition. Together we finished the bottle and talked about things past.

From the beginning it was a catastrophe. I lost two men before we even got near the munition dump. I sent a messenger to Killian to get reinforcements to me so we could put up a good show. The messenger came back to tell me Killian was dead and no one else would take the authority to divert more men to my feint attack. The four of us went in but I could soon tell we weren't drawing any serious fire from the encampment. It wasn't that we hadn't fooled the Japs. They just weren't taking us seriously.

Out of a total of twenty-three men only nine of us got back. Frank wasn't one of them.

During the following weeks rumors persistently trickled in to the effect that Frank had been removed to Cabanatuan, that he was in a prison gang doing road repair work, that he had escaped into the hills. But I was never able to establish the truth.

In early summer I came down with a jungle fever that couldn't even be dignified by the name of malaria. It was simply an enervating, debilitating indifference. High in fever, low in hope; sick in mind, sore in body.

And so I ended my war—on a stretcher headed back to a front-line hospital of the advancing American troops. I was a hero. That's what they told me.

In another month Uncle Sam managed to finish his war without my help.

CHAPTER TWENTY ONE

A thick mahogany beam came into focus, dark and burnished and gleaming with silky smoothness; then thick, wine-colored carpeting, rich oil paintings, a girl kneeling before me. Blue eyes, wet and troubled. Black hair in soft, loose waves.

The war was over—long over. And I was back on Yamata's luxurious yacht with all of this year's headaches rolled into one. I groaned, wondering if Takahito's gun was still buried somewhere in my head. Tulana abruptly raised her head and inspected me as I shifted on the couch.

The worry in her eyes grew deeper. She rose lithely to her feet and moved across the room to a small bar. I closed my eyes, grimly trying to steer a steady course. It was a rough sea. Something cold and wet pushed into my hand. It clinked. I opened my eyes.

"Here. Take this. It will make you feel better."

Nothing in God's world could make me feel worse. I poured it down with a vast thirstiness and handed it back to her.

"That took care of one leg," I croaked.

She frowned. "But I thought it was your head—" Her voice was still soft, still husky.

"Just bring me another, please."

The second drink chased after the first, frightened at being left behind. I lowered the empty glass and looked around.

"Fancy diggings. Morocco bindings on the books. Original Sumaki prints on the walls." I snapped the edge of my glass and listened to the high-pitched ring. "Crystal goblets, too."

I looked at her. At the richly embroidered kimono of heavy silk. "Did I ever tell you about my four years in the stinking jungles of Luzon? We ate any leather we saw. Our prints were maps of enemy gun emplacements. We didn't have any crystal goblets. We dropped on our bellies and sucked up warm water, thick as pea soup, out of the malaria swamps."

"Please, Jim."

"Oh, it wasn't so bad. We never thought about today. Only tomorrow—when everything would be different. Take me, for instance. I kept thinking about that beautiful girl who was waiting for me in Manila. You have no idea how that keeps a guy going. Betrayal, ambush, torture, escape..."

Tulana sat in the chair opposite me, her eyes dull, her face numb and expressionless. With unconscious reflex action she smoothed the silk of her dress over the soft curves of her thighs.

"And then the war was over," I continued, "and Jimmy came marching home. Hurrah, hurrah. But then he got a big, fat jolt. No one was waiting. His friends were drowned. Or shot. Or tortured to death. All because they fought the enemy—the treacherous, stab-in-the-back enemy. And Jimmy's girl friend? Oh yeah. She had married a Japanese colonel. How about that?"

She was crying now; quiet, wracking, shoulder-hunching sobs. I felt empty. A hollow cocoon spun with many dead years. And that made me feel even worse.

"Jim, please!" She lifted her wet face, still managing to cling to that innate sense of dignity that had always, somehow, made her seem so elusive. "You—you wouldn't understand."

"Try me."

"I heard about your attempted escape in the PT boat ... that it was blown up ... that everyone was killed." From somewhere she produced a handkerchief and held it to her face. After a moment, she went on. "It was the end of my world. And I wanted to die, too. You had brought me the world—and then you took it away with you. But ... time goes on. Horribly, at first. Then the pain grows duller, and one realizes what must be—must be. And the Colonel, when he brought the news to me, was so genuinely sorry for me, so attentive. I can't explain it … women are so different from men."

"Yeah," I said flatly.

Tulana went on as though she hadn't heard me. "After the war, we went back to Japan. It was very difficult—the reconstruction period—but the Yamata family was very influential and managed to rebuild their business enterprises quickly. They are in the import and export business …"

"You're telling me!"

"Then, one day, the Colonel admitted he knew you were still alive. That he had known it when we were married. He had read it in some military account of guerrilla activity in the mountains in which your name was mentioned."

She paused, unable to speak for a minute. I went over to the bar and helped myself to another drink. Damned if I wasn't feeling compassion for the Colonel.

"It was terrible. No one should have to die more than once in a lifetime. But I have. And so, more time passed by—filled with the horror of dead hope and cold regret. Then, just a few weeks ago, the Colonel told me we were going to take a long cruise. He said it would be good for me. I didn't know he had this in mind, or even that we were coming to Manila. Jim, you've got to believe me!"

There was nothing to say. I was as empty as my glass.

As she went over to the bar to fix me a refill, I heard a door close softly. A trifle bleary, I turned my head and saw Colonel Yamata enter the salon. His opaque eyes followed Tulana with noncommittal blankness while she delivered my drink and turned to leave the salon, murmuring that she would have some food sent in to me. I couldn't help admiring her departure. The curves were more mature, warmer than I remembered. And I remember well.

Colonel Yamata eyed me with a different interest as he fitted a cigarette into a carved jade holder and twirled it between his fingers with a thoughtful expression.

"Mr. Sheridan," he said, delicately inhaling the scented smoke, "I am certain you have a full appreciation of the situation by now. One might even say you are checkmated."

"One might!"

"Of course, it is now quite useless to point out that your cooperation would never have been needed had you not hidden the treasure with such admirable thoroughness."

I made no comment.

"And the fact that you are the only living man who knows the location of the treasure makes you quite indispensable to me."

I stared at him over the rim of my empty glass and stopped chewing ice cubes.

"So you told me. But how do you figure that one? Several knew besides me."

"Your selection of the past tense, Mr. Sheridan, is quite correct. Shortly after your melodramatic escape in the PT boat we found Karl Fischer. He had washed up on the beach. And he was in very serious condition. Of course, at that time I had no idea how important it was to keep him alive long enough to divulge where the silver was hidden.

"Swede Anderson, as you know, was captured at Bontoc where we just barely missed both you and Frank Stanek. Unfortunately, he proved quite stubborn in spite of our attempts at persuasion. But then, our techniques were very elementary at that time.

"Frank Stanek? He was taken at Appari when your guerrilla gang blew up the munitions dump. Before I could get there, he managed to escape from the prison camp by blowing up a guard tower with a home-made bomb made of cast-iron pipe. Killed four guards. However, a report of his death reached me several months later."

The fact of Frank Stanek's death was difficult to accept. He always seemed the indestructible sort. "What happened to Hernando?" I pursued. "We couldn't find him after our boat was blown up."

The Colonel shrugged indifferently. "Neither did we. But we didn't waste much time searching for him. Undoubtedly, he went down with your boat."

I struggled up and mixed myself another drink. A bit unsteady on my feet, I decided the yacht was rocking. It couldn't be me. But when I looked at the Colonel, he was rocking too.

"One thing I don't get. How come—with all the resources at the command of the Imperial Japanese military—you didn't make extensive efforts to relocate the treasure?"

He smiled thinly. "Believe me, Mr. Sheridan, I made every effort to interest them in doing just that. Unfortunately, the official Japanese occupation currency had suffered so severely under the onslaught of smuggled pesos that the High Command greatly feared any further dilution. Also, we soon needed all available divers in more urgent areas. The salvage operation was discontinued."

"Boomeranged, eh Colonel?"

"I am not certain I follow you."

"Sure you do. It required far more silver pesos to rock the market than a few divers could smuggle in their shoes. You were very clever, Colonel. You and General Tonoya were in cahoots—dumped a hundred times as much on the market as we did. Did it in a deliberate effort to sabotage the diving operation with the idea of coming back after the war and getting it for yourselves. Never figger … figured … that you wouldn't be able to find it again. And thass why you let us get away with goldbricking on the job. Hah! An' we thought we were being clever!"

He continued to survey me lazily, his face floating eerily in a cloud of smoke. Or was I floating? I was ninety-nine point forty-four per cent pure.

"Now, after thirteen years, you're back. Why so long?"

His voice came out of the smoke. "The post-war period was quite difficult. It took much hard work to get back to—this." He waved his cigarette in a loose circle, indicating the luxuriously-appointed ship. "And also I found you extremely difficult to trace. But, believe me, Mr. Sheridan, it was more fascinating than any chess game. When playing for such stakes, time has no meaning."

I dropped more ice cubes into my glass and turned my back to the bar, leaning my elbows against the edge for support.

"Before we get down to business, Colonel, tell me jus' one l'il thing—what kind of an accident happened to General Tonoya?"

He stared at me coldly, as though wondering whether to answer. Apparently he decided it made little difference.

"General Tonoya, unfortunately, suffered a fatal hunting accident at my Maebashi estate. It was most tragic."

"I'll bet."

His answer decided me. If I refused to cooperate, he wouldn't permit me to leave his yacht alive. Even if I did cooperate, my future wasn't much brighter. Well, there were more things at the bottom of Caballo Bay than the Colonel dreamed. Like a mountain of munitions. Just one little revolver could spell the difference.

I had to play along—make it look good—until I could make my bid for escape from this egomaniac.

"Tell me, Colonel, how much does a tub like this cost?"

He had the gleam of ultimate success in his black eyes. Pulling himself up in his chair, he hunched forward for emphasis.

"Made in Japan—about a quarter of a million." He lit another cigarette almost hastily. It was the first sign of emotion I had ever seen in him. "Mr. Sheridan, you will never regret it. I am prepared to give you, as your share of the bargain, the sum of one million dollars!"

Incredulous, I stared at him, my hands clenching themselves into tight, aching knots. Here, smug and self-assured, sat the man who was directly responsible for the deaths of some of the finest men I had ever known. With bland indifference to any feelings I might have harbored over the horrible past, he was offering me a million dollars that wasn't his—if only I would steal the treasure for him.

With an effort, I forced back the sudden red haze that filmed my eyes with hot fury. If ever I needed a cool head, now was the time. Thin-lipped and carefully mechanical, I assured the Colonel I would see him in the morning—ready for diving.

I locked my door and flopped on the bunk without taking off my clothes. The beams of the ceiling spun like helicopter blades, flinging me off into a gray, swirling fog. Then the fog spun itself into the strands of a web and I climbed up and down the thick strands as I tried to escape a huge black-widow spider with slanted eyes. But I couldn't escape. I was bowed down under the load of a million silver pesos. Suddenly the web broke...

Sweat poured from my face and neck as I jerked up and swung my feet onto the floor. I pulled a sodden package of cigarettes from my shirt pocket and shook one out, vacantly noting at the same time that the hands of my watch stood at two o'clock. It was quiet. So quiet that I knew someone was standing in the passageway just outside my door. I could feel it.

Then came a soft, muffled rap. I waited. Again it sounded, urgently. With it, a low whisper, soft as a kitten's breath.

"Jim! Please. Open the door. I must talk with you."

More raps. She waited a long, swelling moment. I buried my face in my hands until I knew she had finally gone. It was over.

Quoth the raven...

I finished my cigarette numbly, feeling as big as an atom in space—or vice versa.

The sun was high and hot when I walked out onto the stern deck the following morning. The Colonel was seated at a table under the awning, his fingers delicately wrapped around a cup of tea. He looked up as I approached. Without turning his head, he motioned to a cabin boy who promptly stepped forward and filled the cup at the place setting opposite him.

"Coffee, Mr. Sheridan," he announced conversationally. "I thought you would prefer it to a cup of tea."

I nodded silently and sat down.

His black eyes rested on mine for a long moment. "I trust you slept well last night?"

Again I nodded silently. I had a queasy feeling in my stomach, but I wasn't sure if it was from last night's drinks, the Colonel, or the prospect of returning to a portion of the nightmarish past—under a hundred and ten feet of water.

"Excellent," he went on. "We should get started as soon as possible. The men have already set up the air compressor and brought out your suit. The equipment is all brand new. I am certain you will find it a vast improvement over that we used during the war."

"No doubt. But haven't you heard of self-contained underwater breathing apparatus?"

"Yes, but I am certain this will be much safer, Mr. Sheridan. And I did not know if you would be familiar with such equipment."

I was familiar with such equipment, all right. And he knew, as well as I did, that it provided much greater mobility. He was taking no chances that I might wander off the premises.

The Colonel was talking.

"...and you will make only a quick preliminary survey this afternoon to determine the exact location of the treasure and mark it with a small buoy. Due to the extra-legal nature of our salvage operation, the actual diving, of course, must be done at night."

Slowly I put my cup down. "Did I hear you right? You expect me to bring up the silver at night—in a hundred feet of water? That's insane!"

"I assure you it is necessary, Mr. Sheridan. But do not be alarmed. You will be equipped with underwater lights. Also, I will provide you with a helper—an ex-navy diver who has had considerable experience."

I wilted back in my chair, speechless. I had planned to spend some time on the ocean floor looking for something other than silver. At best it was a long shot that I could ever relocate a certain box of .45 automatics. But at night. With a Jap diver beside me. I could see my only hope for escape from this nightmare fading away into the darkness of pitch-black water.

"Of course," I said weakly. "I had forgotten. The Philippine government would take a mighty dim view of our enterprise."

Colonel Yamata tapped his mouth with a handkerchief as he gave me a probing look.

"Mr. Sheridan, it is much more serious than that. The government is a minor threat. I thought I had resolved a danger much more deadly, fiendish almost to the point of insanity, but you have convinced me to the contrary. No, Mr. Sheridan—our greatest danger is 'The Barracuda'."

I gaped. "'The Barracuda'?" I echoed inanely. "What is all this business about 'The Barracuda'? What, or who, is it? How does it fit in the picture?"

He settled back with a grim look on his saturnine face, and took a deep breath.

"During the terminal phase of the war—about the time your naval forces attacked Leyte—a mysterious figure became quite active in the Manila Bay area. He operated alone, always protected by the natives who came to regard him as some sort of demi-god. His tactics were horribly efficient. Using frogman equipment, he would move the mines we had placed in the channels and place them in positions that our charts showed to be clear and safe for navigation. You can imagine the catastrophic results. He was utterly diabolical, inhumanly cruel. Troop carriers, battleships, hospital ships—it made no difference to him as long as they were Japanese.

"Every possible trap was laid in an effort to catch him. It was a complete waste of time. He was never caught."

I listened in fascination. "Didn't he reveal himself after the war was over?"

"Never! All we ever learned was that he operated from a base on, or near, the Pasig River—and that he called himself 'The Barracuda'."

"That's a very interesting story. But what has it to do with my diving at night?"

"Very simple, Mr. Sheridan. Somehow, during his activities in Manila Bay, he learned about the vast hoard of silver—and has delivered an ultimatum concerning it."

"Yeah? To whom?"

Silently he opened his cigarette case and handed me a small square of brown paper. It looked like a piece torn from a shopping bag. The printing was in pencil guided by a heavy hand, and equally heavy irony:

"My dearest Colonel,

Kindly send Sergeant Takahito next time—there was so little pleasure in killing your emissary, Mr. Tessa. But he should serve as a clear warning of what will happen to anyone who leaves your yacht—or attempts to salvage silver in Caballo Bay. Go home before it is too late. I would dislike blowing up such a beautiful ship.

The Barracuda"

Automatically, I turned the paper over but there was nothing on the opposite side. I handed it back to the Colonel.

"When did you receive this billet-doux?"

"Early this morning. It was handed to one of the crewmen by an old man on a fishing boat."

"Then you had no opportunity to question the fisherman? To ask him where he got the note?"

He raised a graceful hand, palm upward. "What good would it do? You can be certain that the fisherman knows nothing. As a matter of fact, there is his boat now—just off the tip of Corregidor. He has been fishing ever since he delivered the message."

I shielded my eyes against the bright glare of the sky and looked eastward to where the long, tapered point of the island curled around Caballo Bay. Just offshore, I could make out a small boat bobbing gently in the sea. It was anchored on the course we had taken so many years ago, so many times, from North Dock to the diving barge.

As I observed the familiar scene with hopeless, nameless dread, the yacht engines suddenly sprang to life with a low, muffled roar. In a few moments it had smoothly picked up speed, slicing through the blue water in a graceful, sweeping curve that carried us around the eastern tip of the island and into Caballo Bay. Within twenty minutes we were anchored once more. It appeared to be precisely the spot where the diving barge had once been stationed.

I spent a couple of hours checking out the equipment with the Jap diver and a helper. Everything seemed to be in excellent order. The copper helmet gleamed with newness. The rubberized canvas of the diving suit was white, slightly stiff, still creased from being folded in its packing box. The compressor was the latest word and was powered by an engine that turned over with silky quietness. As I shut it off, Colonel Yamata approached. His excitement was betrayed by a nervously twitching cheek muscle.

"Just in case we are investigated by the coast patrol while you are on the bottom, we have cut loose a spare anchor—and you are attempting to locate it."

I nodded silently, pulling on the suit with the assistance of my Jap helper.

"Do these guys know what they're doing?" I asked, jerking my head toward my silent assistants.

"Of course. Both are very well qualified. As I told you, the diver is an ex-navy man."

"Yeah. Look what happened to your navy." I turned toward him and quickly ran over a few basic signals that would be used in communication between me and the surface. I was relieved to find him alert and experienced. After a few minutes of rehearsal, I turned back to Colonel Yamata.

"Before going down with me, I want to be certain my helper thoroughly understands the signals so we will both use the same ones when we go down together. We can't expect much on the first dive, anyway. It would be a miracle if we found ourselves on exactly the right spot."

The Colonel nodded, accepting this explanation without comment.

"O.K.," I said, motioning for my helmet. "This is it."

The bulbous copper globe dropped into place and was screwed into position. I stood up, feeling the perspiration starting to run from my face and back as the heat trapped in the suit began to parboil me.

As I started toward the ladder, I felt something being pressed into my hand. Startled, I held it up and saw that it was a small figurine of pale, translucent jade. I looked around and saw Tulana watching me with grave, pleading eyes. Immobilized for a moment, I stared until she turned and joined Colonel Yamata in the shade of the awning. Putting the tiny image in my pocket, I started down the ladder.

It was pleasantly different from the last time I had dropped into these cool, green depths. The air came steadily, sweet and pure; the suit was dry and comfortable. Under different circumstances it would have been quite enjoyable. When I hit bottom, however, the terrain was completely unrecognizable. There were the same peaks, dark and rocky. The same white stretches of sand. The same gaudy little fish peering into my helmet with nosy curiosity. But nothing added up to a familiar pattern.

I leaned against the current and pushed my way across the sand, memorizing my route so I could return to the same spot and strike out in another direction if I were unsuccessful the first time. The Colonel would be very upset if he knew I was looking for a pile of scrap instead of a pile of silver.

When I reached the end of my line I returned and started off in another direction at a right angle to my first course. Within fifty feet I noted a familiar rock formation on my left. At the base of it was the covered entrance to the cave in which we had hidden the vast hoard of silver, the treasure of Caballo Bay.

With a grim smile I passed it by and started toward the narrow pass leading to the scrap pile just a few rocky yards away. Then, suddenly, I stood rooted in my tracks.

Gliding down from the top of a small peak, rushing toward me with startling speed, came a strange apparition...a figure with a glass visor over his face, air tanks on his back, flippers on his feet. Propelling himself with powerful thrusts, he dropped to the ocean floor directly in front of me. Under one arm he held a spear gun with easy—yet purposeful—negligence.

I took a step backward in alarm, but with his vastly superior mobility there was nothing to do but wait for his next move.

Slowly and deliberately he advanced, narrowing the sandy distance between us, until I could make out the general configuration of his head. It looked vaguely familiar. Then, behind his faceplate, I could make out cold, narrowed eyes. And his mouth, twisted in a sardonic grin.

Involuntarily I gasped; shocked, disbelieving. It was a ghost. A ghost from the roiling memories of the past. Then a second shockwave hit me with stunning force as I realized intuitively that this mustbe"TheBarracuda" ... mysterious ... ominous ... murderous!

CHAPTER TWENTY TWO

He nodded curtly as I boomed out his name. It echoed dully within the confines of my helmet. Wasting no time on amenities, he pulled a small underwater slate from under his belt, wrote on it quickly and handed it to me with a questioning look.

I read the hurried scrawl: "Ever used SCUBA?"

I looked up with a frown and nodded.

He seized the slate from my hands, erased the question and wrote again, giving precise instructions. We passed it back and forth several times. Each time he waited for my nod of agreement, making certain I understood. As his plan of action became clear, I began to feel a rising pitch of excitement. It was daring, dangerous—but well worth the risk. I couldn't help staring at him as he bent over the slate, wondering what had changed him into this bold, ruthless figure of mystery. It was incredible. A house cat turned to tiger. A bluegill turned to barracuda.

With a sudden effortless shove, he pushed back up to the peak on which he had waited in ambush. He returned in a moment with an extra tank, a pair of flippers and a mask. As he brought them down to me, I felt a brief clutch of panic in my stomach. This would be like trying to ride two motorcycles at once.

The transfer was made without a hitch, however. Freed of my helmet, I quickly pushed the mouthpiece from the air tank into my mouth and then removed the rest of my suit. Next I strapped the air tank on my back, put the faceplate in position, and snapped the flippers in place. Then I motioned for the slate. He watched as I scribbled a brief message and indicated

I wanted to put it into the empty diving suit, which we had weighted down with a small rock. His eyes glinted and he nodded approval after silently moving his lips over the message: "Out to Lunch."

I wasn't feeling very original.

Just before we shoved off I remembered the small jade idol in the pocket of the diving suit. I pulled it out and replaced it in my pants pocket.

We seemed to travel an interminable distance, moving just over the tops of the underwater peaks. Pushing myself to the limit in an effort to keep up with his untiring speed, I soon became hopelessly confused in our direction, completely exhausted at the rapid pace. Just as I was becoming alarmed over the capacity of my air tank, he angled steeply upward into the warmer, sunlit water.

I broke through the surface and found myself beside the weather-beaten hull of a small fishing boat. Jerking away the mouthpiece, I sucked air into grateful lungs and clung to a thick, knotted rope and rested for a moment. It took my last ounce of strength to pull myself up onto the deck, noting with surprise that it was the same fishing boat Colonel Yamata had pointed out to me earlier.

An old man, fishing off the stern, gave me a broken-toothed smile and nodded toward the cabin. It was an unnecessary instruction. I could see the trail of water that led across the deck and disappeared down the hatchway. I removed my equipment while still on deck, idly wondering why my rescuer hadn't done the same. In a moment I followed his wet trail.

Accustomed to the brilliant glare of the tropical sun, my eyes found the cabin in Stygian blackness. His bodyless voice greeted me mockingly.

"Well, Sheridan, it's been a long time, hasn't it?"

His voice was harder than I remembered, controlled and taut.

"I'm glad it wasn't any longer, Morgan," I answered. "How did you know it was I in the diving suit when you dropped off the ledge?"

"Simple matter of probability. I knew you were on the ship. Besides, I had a spear gun in case I guessed wrong." He interrupted himself to shout up the ladder. "Juan! Start the engine. Head back to Manila, *rapidamente!*"

Almost immediately the boat vibrated from the powerful roar of a large engine. As it swelled in volume and we surged forward, I was thrown back against a bulkhead, unprepared for such terrific acceleration.

"We can outrun anything in Manila Bay," Morgan said, answering my unspoken question, "if we find it necessary." I heard the opening of a small, heavy door in the darkness. "How about a drink? I have gin and tonic, or beer."

I took beer. It was cold and I drank thirstily.

Morgan gave a short, barking laugh. "I used to play a game with myself during the war. If a mine I had moved was hit by a warship, I had beer. If it was a troopship I had gin and tonic. If it was a hospital ship I took straight gin."

"What kept you from becoming an alcoholic?"

"Hell, I had no way of knowing what ship would come through next. It was a throw of the dice."

Under a thick covering of drapes, the portholes were dark gray discs, barely admitting enough light for me to see the bottle of beer in my hands. I sensed, rather than saw, that Morgan was huddled in a corner of his bunk, and occasionally I could hear a thick, vibrant twang as if he unconsciously reached out and pulled at the powerful rubber sling of his spear gun while he talked. Except for a brief glimpse through the obscurity of his mask while we were still on the bottom, I had not yet seen his face. In fact, since we came aboard his ship I had not seen him at all. It was eerie. Like talking to the Imp of the Bottle.

"Look," I said, "how about a little light in here? I can't see a damned thing."

"No!" he exploded. "No light." The bunk springs creaked as he leaned forward in alarm. Then he eased back and went on in a lower tone. "It's cooler without light."

It was—like hell was cool.

"How did you know that Yamata had suckered me into a trap?" I asked. "He played a well-hidden game."

His words were dipped in acid and strung out on a line of sarcasm. "I didn't know. When my, ah, agent left the Casa Grande after attending to Tessa, he saw you riding off in a car with our old friend Takahito. He didn't know if you went under duress or of your own free will. But I remembered your many happy hours of chess playing with Colonel Yamata—and I also recalled that you were the one key, beside myself, that could open the secret of the treasure cave. Not knowing whether you were playing for the white or the black, I decided to make a little test."

"A test? What kind of a test?"

"Very simple. When I saw you go over the side of Yamata's ship I decided to meet you on the bottom. If you went for the scrap pile I would know you were looking for a gun. If you started to pull away the rocks from the entrance of the cave—well, you would never have known what hit you!"

I suppressed a shudder. "Sounds a bit arbitrary—if not downright capricious."

"Sheridan, I learned during the war that just one mistake could mean death. I can't afford not to be arbitrary." His voice suddenly rose to a shout as he called to the old fisherman through the hatchway. "Juan! Juan, how are we doing?"

The answer came back in a moment. "They are now following us, Señor Morgan. About two miles distant."

"*Bueno.* You know the course to follow, Juan."

"*Sí.* I know."

I peered into the dark gloom, trying vainly to catch a glimpse of Morgan's face.

"Who is following us? Yamata?"

His answer was smug with self-satisfaction. "Yes. Yamata. And Yamata goes nowhere without Sergeant Takahito. I've baited a trap for our good friends. When they pulled up your empty diving suit they were bound to think of an innocent-looking fishing boat and come in hot pursuit. Without you, the Colonel can never hope to recover the silver." He laughed with thin humor. "If you don't mind the comparison, you are the cheese in the trap."

The comparison didn't delight me. In fact, I was getting a bit sore. Colonel Yamata thought I was a cat's paw. Morgan was even more insulting. I was cheese to catch rats. This wasn't my game in the first place and I didn't care whether the white or the black won. Damned if I was going to be pushed around much longer like an unwilling pawn waiting for the sacrifice play.

"So they walk into a trap. So what?"

"What do you think? I've waited thirteen years for this day, Sheridan. Thirteen long years to even up the score with Takahito. I had just about given up. I was even planning a trip to Japan to find him, praying I'd find him in good health. But now he is back. And I'm going to make him suffer, just like he has made me suffer through all these years. Like I will suffer until the day I die. Getting Yamata at the same time will make it all the sweeter."

The venom in his voice bit into me like a corrosive acid. I could feel a prickly sensation crawling up my spine as I began to realize he was completely mad. All the valiant deeds of the war had not stemmed from any sense of patriotism. They sprang from some twisted, crazy conception of himself as a God-image. From a remote, egocentric pinnacle of insanity he was the avenging angel and the killer of the sea all rolled into one—a demented barracuda.

My mind raced in an effort to find some scheme of action. I had a warm feeling that I was in the fire without the frying pan. He talked on.

"Back on that day, when Takahito cut my air hose, I didn't really comprehend the horror of what had happened to me. I thought it was only a temporary case of the bends. At the hospital they applied all sorts of crude treatment. I became a human guinea pig for every crackpot idea they could dream up. But instead of being cured, I got worse. After two years of this it dawned on me that I was permanently crippled, that it was useless to hope I would ever be normal again.

"They finally relegated me to the human rubbish pile, not even bothering to put me under guard. In the first place, I could scarcely walk and in the second, what the hell could I do if I did escape?"

The boat suddenly careened over on its side and I clutched for support. We began to weave back and forth in a violent series of maneuvers. The sound of the engine echoed hollowly as our zigzag course led between larger ships and I knew we were approaching the crowded area near the mouth of the Pasig River. We slowed down, made several sharp turns, then speeded up again. Apparently we were giving our pursuers enough time to keep up with us without making them suspicious that they were being lured into a trap.

After a few minutes the engine was again throttled down and we seemed to be picking our way through a narrow channel, teeming with smaller craft. The odor of the river seeped into the cabin, a devil's perfume of rot, garbage and filth.

Morgan gave a satisfied grunt and determinedly continued his story, as if he were trying to sell the rights to me.

"A Filipino nurse, who hated the Japs almost as much as I, helped me to escape. One night she managed to smuggle me from the hospital in a laundry truck to her father—Juan—who had this fishing boat on the river. It was an ideal hiding place. I spent my time learning to speak Spanish. When we went out to sea, and were far from shore where no one could see me, I would crawl out onto the deck and try to help Juan with his fishing. You can imagine the beauty of my life, the bright hope, the shining future. Each morning when I woke up, I died all over again.

"Then, one day, Juan brought me a frogman's outfit. It was a birthday present. I threw it at him, cursed him. But a week later I tried it on late at night when Juan was asleep and dropped into the water. As I went deeper and deeper a miracle happened! My legs straightened out, my arms unbent, and I felt like a normal human being again—no, more than that—a god, a god of the sea. The pressure of the water had done what no doctor in Manila had been able to do. Can you imagine the shock when I came up out of the water and found I was the same as before—a crawling, scuttling wreck? I cried like a baby.

"But, from then on I lived in the water. Did everything but sleep in it. Manila Bay became as familiar as the palm of my hand. And even more wonderful—I found my revenge. By moving their own mines into the paths of their ships I damned near forced the Japs to abandon Manila Bay. I sank so many I quit keeping score. And the natives began to help, to bring me information. They treated me with respect. I was somebody. I had a close scrape with a Jap officer once, but when he came to see me with a squad of soldiers he just laughed. Instead of 'The Barracuda,' he said he had found a lobster. But it didn't hurt. In fact, I felt a strange, weird pride.

"But then the war was over and the Japs went home. I was lost, left in a vacuum. Oh, I could have anything in the world I wanted. The resources of the silver treasure were at my command, but I took only enough for necessities. What would I do with anymore? Buy big cars, a mansion, entertain pretty girls? The sight of me made people sick. No matter how hard they tried to hide it, I could see it in their eyes. After my days of glory it was hard to take."

He stopped and gave a short laugh, "This is getting to be quite a monologue. Want another beer?"

"No," I answered curtly. "Let's hear the rest of it." I had to admit I was fascinated with his horrible tale.

He chopped out another laugh. "You're a glutton for punishment. Well ... for the finale to this Homeric legend ...

"One day, not too long ago, a high official in the HUK movement, which," he added parenthetically, "has been driven underground, as you know, came to visit me. He explained to me what they were doing and what they planned for the islands. Because of my reputation and standing with the natives he wanted my help. The name of 'The Barracuda' had become a popular symbol of resistance, of patriotism, of love for the common man. It would serve as a rallying point to give the HUKs a cohesion they had never had.

"And what this guy had to say made sense. The common man had gained nothing from the glorious new independence of the Philippines. He had fought for it—but the rich still owned it, and were getting richer. The poor still got nothing but babies. Why not chop up the plantations and divide them among the have-nots? Instead of working for fat, absentee owners who sunned themselves on the Riviera, they could work for themselves. There would be no burden of capital ownership. Until they could handle that responsibility everyone would work for the state. The children would have the tradition—and corruption—of the past cut away from them. By removing them from their parents and educating them in state schools they would learn to fight for a greater Philippines and, ultimately, share their rightful place in the sun ..."

Seeing the direction of this baloney, I couldn't restrain myself from interrupting.

"That crap has a familiar ring to it. I've heard it all before. I can hardly believe that you are really buying it."

Instead of taking offense, he gave a sour laugh. "I guess I didn't expect you'd understand, Sheridan. You've sucked in too much propaganda for too many years to be able to sift wheat from chaff. And it's a pity. I hoped you would see things our way. But it makes no difference, anyway. Regardless of how you feel about it—you are going to help me. The treasure of Caballo Bay is mine. I have earned it with years of pain and suffering. Now I am going to make certain that it will be used to bring a new order to the Philippines, a new order in which I will be important once more—the power behind the throne!"

His concluding outburst was punctuated by a final coughing wheeze of the engine, and the fishing boat bumped against some solid object and stopped moving. Through the heavily curtained hatchway I could hear faint sounds of children laughing, dogs barking, men shouting for the right of way as they pushed their boats along the crowded river. It was the sound of the Pasig River, the crowded home to teeming thousands who lived out their lives on tiny cascos on the water or in ramshackle huts along the banks.

Juan came down the ladder slowly, his bent figure casting a shadow on the curtain as he stopped on the bottom step.

"We have arrived, Señor Morgan," he announced. "They are only a few minutes behind us."

"*Bueno*, Juan," Morgan answered, his voice rising with tension. "You may leave now."

The old man hesitated, shifting uncertainly. "Perhaps it is best that I stay, Señor Morgan."

Morgan spoke sharply. "No. I can handle things very well. Do not worry, I will see you later, Juan."

As Juan reluctantly turned and climbed the ladder, my seething irritation came to an explosive boil.

"Morgan," I gritted, "if you think I'm going to sit here like a lamb tied to a rope, you're a helluva lot crazier than I think you are. First, Yamata tries to push me around in his game. Now you're trying to push me around in yours. Well, James B. Sheridan is going to play his own game from now on—and it doesn't include cold-blooded murder." I rose to my feet, anger tightening my muscles. "Who the devil do you and Yamata think you are, anyway, that you can operate outside all the laws of the civilized world? He is mad with greed, but you're even worse— you are mad with hate, with revenge, with self-pity. Do you think shooting Takahito will give you back what you have lost? Thousands of guys lost more than you did in the war and they're managing to live with themselves. It looks like they've got something you haven't got—plain, old-fashioned guts."

As I paused for breath I heard a sudden, ominous click. The sound of a hammer pulled back on a pistol. With it came Morgan's voice, low and tight.

"You shouldn't have said that, Sheridan. I wasn't sure what I would do with you … after this is over. But now I know where you stand. You're no different than the rest. You despise me because I'm crippled!"

I was moving silently toward the heavily-curtained hatchway. I had to make a break for it. To warn Colonel Yamata of the trap.

"Now I'll have to kill you, too." His voice squeezed to a higher pitch. "Because if I don't …"

Suddenly my foot hit against a pail with a rasping clatter and he screamed hysterically, "Don't move! Don't move or I'll shoot! Get back. Over there in front of the porthole."

I moved back to where my head was silhouetted against the gray disc of light. He laughed raucously. My hand touched the coarse fabric draped over the porthole. Beads of perspiration trickled down my forehead. Now I knew what it was like to face a firing squad.

"Pretty as a cameo, Sheridan," he said with heavy irony. "Now you are going to see 'The Barracuda' in action. And that is a real honor, because no one ever has."

Abruptly he fell silent as a heavy thump on the deck above us rocked the small boat sharply. A second, lighter thump followed.

"Make a sound," he whispered with savage urgency, "and you get it right in the belly."

Soft steps moved across the deck with hesitant slowness. Then, warily, they sounded on the ladder. One cautious, exploratory step. Another. Then another. I couldn't yell a warning if I tried. My throat felt paralyzed. My heart was playing hopscotch.

With a sudden, bull-like lunge, the squat figure of Sergeant Takahito stormed past the curtain and dove into the cabin. Jumping away from the light of the hatchway, he backed up against the wall. Dimly I could make out the gun that he held up with uncertain direction, waiting for his eyes to accustom themselves to the murky gloom of the cabin. I could almost touch him.

"Well, well," Morgan suddenly cackled shrilly. "If it isn't my old pal, Sergeant Takahito. Welcome aboard, my friend."

Frightened and uncomprehending, Takahito jerked his head about, trying to locate Morgan's position. His gun swept in an erratic arc.

"Morgan, you fool!" I found my voice, but I didn't recognize it. Ragged, sharp as a broken bottle. "He doesn't understand English, remember? Your big revenge deal is falling flat. He doesn't even know who you are!"

At the sound of my voice, Takahito swung his gun toward me. He was beginning to panic. It was enough to unnerve anybody. Jeering voices, angry voices. Pitch blackness. A feeling of madness in the air.

With Morgan's insane laughter booming in the narrow confines of the cabin, I saw the tall, spare figure of Colonel Yamata step through the hatchway. He pushed aside the curtain with easy indifference and stood framed against the bright rectangle of light. As if he were looking for the headwaiter in a nightclub.

"Sheridan!" he snapped coolly. "Are you in there?"

"Yeah…"

Morgan broke in, his voice heavy with perverted humor. "You bet he is, Colonel. Come in and join our party. I've been waiting a long time to give you a proper welcome."

It was impossible to tell if Colonel Yamata was at all surprised. He was just a black silhouette. But his tone was as controlled as always.

"So! Mr. Morgan Montgomery. Alias 'The Barracuda,' if I deduce correctly?"

"Brilliant!" Morgan sneered. "Too bad you didn't deduce before it was too late."

"Too late, Mr. Montgomery? I'm afraid I don't understand."

"Yes, too late!" Morgan's voice rose in pitch, cracking off-key. I caught my breath as I heard him shifting position on his bunk. "Too late, my dear Colonel, to steal the treasure of Caballo Bay. Too late to save your butcher boy, Takahito. Too late to escape. Tell him, Sheridan. Tell him in Japanese so Takahito will understand why he is going to die!" The words spilled out, feverishly, hysterically.

"Morgan!" I shouted. "Don't do it!"

"Tell him!" he screamed. "Tell him."

Takahito didn't understand the words, but he must have felt the venomous hate that poured from Morgan like sulphuric acid. He suddenly bent over in a half crouch and aimed his gun in final decision. At the same moment I gripped the drapes behind me and ripped them from the porthole. Sunshine burst in like a brilliant floodlight, pouring over the bunk on which a strange apparition was huddled. I made a desperate lunge for the spear gun which Morgan held to his shoulder.

I was too late. He screamed in mad rage, releasing the trigger, then flung his arms up against the blinding glare. The spear hit the opposite cabin wall with a heavy thud. I turned and looked, horrified. It had drilled clear through Takahito's chest, impaling him like a mounted beetle. His eyes swelled in their sockets and a gurgling cry pushed through his lips. With a tremendous effort he sighted the gun on Morgan's twisted body and pulled the trigger. The shots boomed like thunder. The first burned through my side with searing heat and I dropped to the floor. Two more shots followed in quick succession, one hitting an empty beer bottle with a shattering crash, and the last catching Morgan directly between the eyes.

It had taken but a few seconds, and then a deathly silence filled the cabin. Colonel Yamata still stood in the hatchway as though paralyzed. Slowly he focused on the slumped body of Takahito, unbelieving, uncomprehending. Then, with an agonized cry he fell to the floor and grasped a limp hand, cupping it between his own.

I crawled to my feet, clutching my ripped side. One look at Morgan and I knew it was useless to check for a pulse. The days of 'The Barracuda' were over. I turned away and stiffened in numbed surprise. Colonel Yamata was kneeling on the floor, staring at me with tears glistening on his cheeks. Clutched in both hands was Takahito's gun. It was aimed at my chest.

I shook my head tiredly, beyond fear. Almost beyond caring.

"You can't do it, Colonel. For fifteen years you've played a ruthless, cunning game. You've swept all the pieces from the board, thinking you'd end up with the balance of power—but it hasn't worked out. Your power died with Takahito. Now we're the only two left on the board. It's a stalemate."

Slowly I moved past him. He held the gun trained on the spot where I had been standing, his eyes vacant. I shoved through the curtain over the hatchway and moved, one painful step at a time, up the ladder into the bright, warm sunlight. I gained the deck and started for the rail. A muffled explosion sounded from the cabin below. The game was over.

No one paid the slightest bit of attention to the spreading crimson blotch under my arm as I stepped off the fishing boat onto the rotted wooden pilings of the wharf. On the Pasig River one minds one's own business.

After twenty painful minutes of searching, I found a telephone at a small grocery store and called Costeau.

"Come and get me," I gasped. "I'm down here between the pineapples and the rutabagas."

CHAPTER TWENTY THREE

Costeau made me tell him the whole story from beginning to end, listening with enthralled intensity, interrupting now and then for elaboration here, more explanation there.

"And that's it," I finally concluded, completely talked out.

"*Mon dieu!*" he exclaimed, his mustaches quivering with excited frustration. "How I envy you! Such excitement! Such adventure!" He smacked a huge fist into his other hand. "If only I could have been with you."

I groaned. Nobody knew the trouble I'd seen.

He gave my bandaged side a solicitous look. "Ah. It hurts badly? There is something I can do?"

This was more like it.

"Uh huh. The sun is in my eyes."

"But of course. We have talked so long. I am so inconsiderate."

He promptly picked me up, wicker chair and all, and carried me further into the shade. Then he lifted my feet, slid the footstool back in position, and moved the table close to my elbow.

"And now, perhaps something to eat? A cantaloupe? Papaya? Some black Malaga grapes?"

"No," I answered weakly. "Perhaps a bit more gin and tonic, though. It seems to give me strength."

He attended to this by shouting at Carlos, who was posted on the veranda in case I should need attention.

"And some cigarettes," I added.

Jacques bellowed this instruction to the retreating figure of Carlos, then turned back to me.

"I think, perhaps I shall have to replace Carlos. He is beginning to look a little exhausted."

"Yes." I, for one, understood sympathy. "He doesn't move nearly as fast as he did this morning. I hope I'm not causing too much trouble."

"But certainly not," he hastily reassured me. "And I am certain you are in a great hurry to get well again—so you can dive for the treasure, eh?"

I shook my head. "Jacques, I wouldn't touch it with a hundred-and-ten-foot pole. It has maimed and murdered. Destroyed and twisted and hurt both the greedy and the innocent. It should now be allowed to rest in peace at the bottom of the sea where it can do no more harm. No, I'll have no more to do with it."

He was aghast. "But, *mon ami,* over fifteen million pesos are still there. A magnificent fortune. Part of it could be yours. And you are the only one who knows where it is. You will never be allowed to rest until you have divulged the secret."

I sighed with exasperation. "Jacques. Even you. I'm beginning to think I am the only normal human left in this greedy world."

"In this world, my friend, the normal are abnormal."

"Even if I were interested, which I am not, it would cost a great deal to set up a salvage operation."

"But I have already talked with my cousin. He is on the Board of Directors of the Bank of Manila. They will be happy to provide you with all the necessary equipment—and give you ten per cent of the salvage value, besides."

"You rogue, I'll never teach you how to play chess. The answer is still no."

He stood up, acknowledging defeat with a massive shrug. Although he would gain nothing if I decided to salvage the silver, his prudent mind reeled at the waste. Maybe I wasn't normal, after all.

"Very well, *mon ami.* It is you who must make the decision," he said sadly. "No one else has the right to interfere."

The first kind words I had heard in a long time. James B. Sheridan was no pawn to be pushed around.

With slumping shoulders he walked heavily across the courtyard and stepped up onto the tile terrace. As he approached the doorway, Ellen dashed through, halted at the sight of his defeated figure and held a hurried consultation with him. I couldn't make out their words. In a moment she came skipping around the pool, wrapping me in a big dimpled smile.

"Well, Diego," she greeted me. "How is our patient today?"

"Our patient thinks he is dying," I answered morosely.

Her warm brown eyes twinkled. "But you never looked better."

"And I never felt worse."

"So brave. So noble. Like the Spirit of '76."

"Racked with pain. Besieged with the winds of adversity. Like the Spirit of St. Louis."

"Well," she said, giving my empty glass a stern look. "Maybe you're just as high."

"Humpf!"

She sat down on the footstool and regarded me with a serious expression. "Diego, everyone feels low at times..."

"Thought you just said I was high."

"Especially at times when you seem to have finished a chapter in your life," she went on, ignoring me, "and things have come to a dead end. You become confused and lose your sense of direction. Life becomes a senseless vacuum. I know. I felt that way before I came to Manila and took this job."

"I felt that way after," I muttered.

"But everything has worked out so beautifully. I've met the finest, most wonderful people, like Jacques Costeau, and all the other new friends I now have. And you. Life has taken on a new meaning for me."

"So you think that if I salvaged the treasure, life would take on a new meaning for me, too?"

She dimpled at me again. "Yes. And you would be rich. And be able to marry me. And we would live happily ever after."

"You're a greedy little gold-digger." I couldn't help grinning.

"Silver-digger," she corrected. Then her eyes became round and grave. "Jim, I don't care if you don't keep a single peso. It doesn't mean a thing to me. But that silver belongs to the people of Manila who entrusted their savings to the bank—it means a great deal to them. All the little shopkeepers, the small farmers, the people who are trying to build better lives for themselves."

"You forgot the poor widows," I added, carried away by the spirit of the thing, the Spirit of '76, and the Spirit of St. Louis.

"Oh, how can you be so, so callous?" She spun around on the stool and excavated in a pocket for a handkerchief. I held mine out and she snatched it from my hand without a word.

Leaning back in my chair, full of contrition and gin, I heard a shout from the veranda.

"Hey! I hear somebody is looking for the world's best diver!"

I snapped my head around and gaped in delighted amazement.

"Frank! Frank Stanek. Where in God's name did you come from?"

He sauntered toward me with a nonchalant grin, making it seem that we had just parted a few hours ago. If it wasn't the same old bulldog pipe, it was one just as worthy of cremation. And he was the same Frank, with just a bit more gray in his crewcut hair.

The next hour was quite confused as we caught up on the long years that separated us. Costeau reappeared with a large tray of potables and stayed to join the party. Ellen also stayed, warming Frank with her biggest smile and the best of gin. It was quite an afternoon.

"But how did you know I was here?" I finally asked as we talked our way back to the present. "I just arrived three days ago."

He grinned, rubbing the bowl of his pipe along his jaw.

"Damndest thing," he said. "I had read about a gold strike on the island of Mindoro just a couple of weeks ago. I quit my job down in Sarawak where I was managing a copra plantation, bought myself a little boat and came north. The strike didn't amount to anything and I was just barely making expenses when this guy came up to me with a message. Said it was from you. I was supposed to hustle back to Manila where you and I were going to salvage the silver of Caballo Bay. Christ, was I surprised! I thought it had been salvaged long ago. I was even more surprised to hear you had negotiated the deal with the Bank of Manila."

I glared at Ellen and Costeau, but they were obviously as mystified as I.

"Well, this guy—I think he was a Jap—led me back to Manila Bay and took me out to the most beautiful yacht I have ever seen. Sleek, trim, painted all white. And there I got another shock. I was met by the most beautiful gal I've ever laid eyes on."

"Sleek and trim and painted," Ellen meowed softly in my ear.

Frank continued, not hearing her comment. "And she turns out to be this girl, Tulana. The one that you…" He suddenly paused and cleared his throat delicately, giving Ellen a sidelong glance.

"Yes," I said hastily, "I remember."

"Well, uh, she tells me that her husband, Colonel Yamata, had committed suicide under very tragic circumstances and that she is going away somewhere. Wants to rebuild her life. Wouldn't mind helping her, come to think of it. Anyway, she doesn't want to keep anything that will remind her of the past. She said the past owed her something, however."

"Like what?" I demanded, a bit truculent.

"Like the treasure of Caballo Bay, which had caused so much suffering, should now be used to bring some good, some happiness, into the world."

"Oh."

"Also she said she knew you'd never accept anything from her but she wanted her yacht, and all its diving equipment, to be used for this purpose. So she's going to give it to me."

"What!"

He grinned and lifted his glass with a gesture of worldly *savoir faire*. "That's right. As far as I'm concerned, the past doesn't owe me a thing—but she begged so pitifully that I couldn't refuse."

"Noble soul!"

"I'm supposed to go back out to the ship tonight," he went on, "when she'll have the deed of ownership ready. But, of course, the whole thing is contingent on you."

Although he made his tone light, I could see that, deep underneath, it meant a great deal to him.

"Contingent on me? How come?"

Carefully he stoked his pipe. "Very simple. If you won't throw in with me, or me with you, the whole business is called off."

"We don't need her ship."

"No. But she wants it that way. Sort of an atonement, I guess. And maybe you owe *her* something—from the past."

I took a deep breath and glanced at their sober, expectant faces. Was I too stubborn? Stupidly stubborn? In my grim determination not to be a pawn, shoved around by the whim of circumstance, I had lost sight of an obvious fundamental—we are all pawns shoved around on the board of fate. Colonel Yamata was pushed by his own greed. Morgan by blind hate. Frank by a narcotic love for adventure. No one could escape this eternal interplay.

"All right," I answered resignedly. "I give up. I'm beat."

"No, my friend," Costeau shouted in elation. "You are just beginning to play the game! And this, we celebrate. Carlos! Wake up. Bring champagne. Quickly."

I grinned. It was worth it just for the big, warm kiss Ellen planted on my lips.

Frank probed in the depths of an inside pocket and handed me a large envelope.

"Here," he said. "Tulana said to give this to you if you would agree to dive for the treasure. It is something else she wants no more part of."

I ripped it open. The contents consisted of a very legal-looking document with a cover letter attached. In dry terms it informed me that I was now sole owner of all the assets of the Great Western Importing Company.

Frank grinned at the startled look on my face. "I don't know what she meant by it, but Tulana said it was the trap that brought you back into the game—and since you had won the game, the spoils belonged to you."

I wasn't often speechless, but this stopped me for a moment. Dredging deep into my pocket, I pulled up a tiny jade figurine and handed it to Frank.

"Here," I said. "When you go back to the ship tonight will you return this to her? Tell her it worked its charm."

He laid it in the palm of his hand and looked at it curiously. "What is it?" he asked.

"Kuan Yin," I answered. "The God of Compassion."

It was late before we finished dinner. Costeau had gone about his business of innkeeping. Frank, with a light in his eye, had left for the sleek yacht in Manila Bay. Ellen, realizing that I was still a bit weak, made me promise to go up to my room early in spite of my protests that I wanted to hear her sing.

As I reached the foot of the stairway, a sudden thought occurred to me. I turned and went back to the desk where Wong, the desk clerk, was sorting mail.

"I want to send a cablegram," I said.

"Certainly, Mr. Sheridan." He seized a pad and waited with poised pencil.

"To Mr. Julius Wharton. Great Western Importing Company. San Francisco, California."

"Yes, sir."

I stared at the ceiling, then went on: "Have assumed ownership of Great Western Importing Company. Your position as general manager still secure. Please watch expenses."

"Is that all, Mr. Sheridan?"

"Yup. Oh, just one more thing." I gave him the hard-boiled look befitting a new owner.

"Send it collect."

THE END

www.ingramcontent.com/pod-product-compliance
Lightning Source LLC
Chambersburg PA
CBHW031319280626
47169CB00019B/2239